The Complete Book of
Mosaics

The Complete Book of
Mosaics

Techniques and Instructions
for Over 25 Beautiful Home Accents

Emma Biggs and Tessa Hunkin

The Reader's Digest Association, Inc.
Pleasantville, NY/Montreal/Sydney

A READER'S DIGEST BOOK

This edition published by The Reader's Digest Association, Inc.,
by arrangement with Breslich & Foss, Ltd.

CONCEIVED AND PRODUCED BY
BRESLICH & FOSS LTD., LONDON
Photography: Shona Wood
Templates: Stephen Dew
Design: Janet James
Production: Paula Osborne
Project Management: Janet Ravenscroft

FOR READER'S DIGEST

U.S. Project Editor: Susan Randol
Canadian Project Editor: Pamela Johnson
Copy Editor: Marcy Gray
Project Designer: George McKeon
Executive Editor, Trade Publishing: Dolores York
Associate Publisher, Trade Publishing: Christopher T. Reggio
President & Publisher, Trade Publishing: Harold Clarke

Library of Congress Cataloging-in-Publication Data

Biggs, Emma, 1956-
The complete book of mosaics: techniques and instructions
for over 25 beautiful home accents / by Emma Biggs and
Tessa Hunkin.
    p. cm.
Includes index.
ISBN 0-7621-0613-1
1. Mosaics—Technique. 2. House furnishings.
3. Garden ornaments and furniture. I.
Hunkin, Tessa, 1954- II. Title.

TT910.B5296 2005
738.5—dc22   2004061482

Address any comments about
The Complete Book of Mosaics to:
    The Reader's Digest Association, Inc.
    Adult Trade Publishing
    Reader's Digest Road
    Pleasantville, NY 10570-7000

For more Reader's Digest products and information,
visit our website:

    www.rd.com (in the United States)
    www.readersdigest.ca (in Canada)
    www.readersdigest.au (in Australia)

Printed in Hong Kong

1 3 5 7 9 10 8 6 4 2

Contents

Introduction

Our aim in this book is to provide you with the information you need to make mosaics. First, there's a general section that describes all of the mosaic materials, tools, and techniques you will come across, with explanations of their different properties and applications. This is followed by an exciting range of projects—for both indoor and outdoor locations—that show these different applications in step-by-step detail.

We have been working as professional mosaicists for more than fifteen years, and in this book we pass on to you the benefit of our experience as we describe the process of both designing and making a project. You will find detailed information, as well as a range of templates, which will enable you to recreate the projects illustrated. Readers who don't plan to make these specific projects will still find useful hints that can be applied to their own work.

Mosaic is about making pictures and patterns from hundreds of separate elements, and the art of successful mosaic is to create order and harmony out of chaos. This can be a challenge, but it can also be very rewarding. We hope that you will get as much pleasure from it as we have over the years.

Emma Biggs and Tessa Hunkin

the techniques

Design essentials

Mosaic is a medium of wide expressive possibilities. It is a playful art form, and its material is seductive. Its history is a history of decoration. If you look at examples from mosaic's grandest, most significant historical moments, such as the mosaics in early Christian cathedrals (that tell stories from the Bible and use gold to symbolize divine light), it is easy to see that the mosaics do not dominate, but work alongside, other art forms. Mosaic is inseparable from the architecture it graces. But if the medium is playful, it is also practical. A gold dome might suggest heaven, but it also helps lighten a dark space. A mosaic pavement in a Roman villa might be a decorative flourish that suggests the function of the room, but it is also a cool and practical surface for a floor.

As you start work in a new medium, it is hard not to be influenced by its history. The playful nature of mosaic is liberating, but as with any form it is not entirely without rules. Some of these rules are useful to know, and may help even the freest of approaches. In this book, the introduction to each project sketches out the design principles involved—including issues of color—so this section provides an overview of the more general points you should consider.

Below In this deceptively simple pattern, bright orange tiles are a vivid counterpoint to the yellow-greens and blue-grays. The design uses quarter-cut vitreous glass tiles.

Pattern

Mosaic is made up of a collection of units: the mosaic tiles, or "tesserae." Pattern is inherent to mosaic to some degree, as the repeated elements—the tiles—create a pattern, whether or not this is your primary intention. If tiles are put together in a visually satisfying way, the system can be repeated, creating a pattern within a pattern. This can be done in a geometric way for one kind of effect (see the Striped Backsplash on p. 110) or in an asymmetrical way for another (for example, the Patio Table on p. 106). Pattern can also be a matter of symmetry (see the Bird Mirror

Frame on p. 44). Something that looks tediously repetitious as a pencil drawing can turn out to be incredibly complex and aesthetically pleasing when made in a variety of colors and mosaic materials.

Symmetry or asymmetry, geometric repeats, color, surface, and texture can all be used as elements in pattern-making. With so many variables at your disposal, it helps to limit choice. Very successful designs can be made using a single color or a single kind of cut. The fact that mosaic involves pattern as a secondary effect can cause problems.

Sometimes the mosaicist is so concerned with the principal motif that he or she doesn't notice other kinds of patterns developing—and some of these can be hard to spot at first. A classic mosaic fault is to have tiles running in and out of sync with one another. Unintentional grids in the alignment of tiles and lines crashing into one another can spoil an otherwise pleasing design. Once you have an eye for these problems, you can spot them even in the work of professional mosaicists.

Above The simplest patterns are "random" mixes of colors, such as the three examples shown here. However, pure chance is unlikely to produce an even spread of bright, "accent" colors. Help chance along by distributing the brightest tiles evenly across the whole design.

Texture and Surface

Vitreous glass and unglazed ceramic tiles have slightly different surface finishes that can add a lively look to your design, although they have no particular textural interest. Marble can be used for its glassy polished face, or riven (cut with an unfinished broken surface) for its textural qualities. Found materials can be combined with traditional mosaic materials to good effect. A school of mosaic design has developed (following the example of British mosaicist Jane Muir) in which materials with different textures are arranged in rows, often in combination with slate, pebbles, or gold and silver. This is very effective and good for the beginner, particularly if the choice of colors is deliberately limited.

The drama of the properties of texture and surface (the difference between matte and shiny tiles, for example) is sadly ignored by many professional mosaicists. The Memory Tile (p. 59), Dragonfly Panel (p. 62), Mirrored Sconce (p. 81) and Textured Panel (p. 126) all address these issues. When it comes to displaying textured mosaics, overhead light is hard and unflattering, creating unpleasant shadows. Oblique light brings out the best in textural designs. A textural mosaic is most effective hung on a north wall in natural light.

Below This wall panel uses found objects of varying shapes and textures. The arrangement of color adds additional depth to the design.

Below This striking design uses riven marble in muted shades and brightly colored smalti (see p. 25). Its texture is perfect in an outdoor setting.

Cutting and Spacing

The practical side of cutting is discussed on pp. 14 and 15 of this book, but there is another element to cutting that is not often made clear to the beginner. The most crucial aspect of creating an attractive mosaic is not how you cut the tiles, but how you lay them. You can see this vividly demonstrated by looking at mosaics made with uncut tiles. The mosaicist's skills (or lack of them) can make a wall of uncut mosaic look seamlessly elegant or a complete mess, depending on the attention paid to the joints—the space between the individual tiles. The same is true for cut-piece mosaic. An attractive mosaic can be made from the scraps on the floor after a day's cutting: mosaic works if the spacing is right.

Spacing is like the time signature in music or tension in knitting: once you have decided on what the spacing should be (it can be tight, or wide, or something in between), stick with it. Of course, you can structure differences of spacing into a design, but the piece will have much greater visual coherence if the eye can clearly see that the differences are intentional. A few pieces of leftover tile shoved in to fill inconvenient holes tend not to look intentional, no matter how much the mosaicist wishes they did.

Above The direction of laying, scale, and spacing are all issues at work in this panel made from unglazed ceramic. Broken tiles and random shapes are arranged into a sampler of different effects.

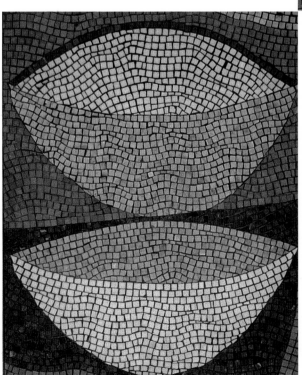

Left This marble panel shows an interesting way to use lines of coursing. The lines run from left to right across the design, which lends a feeling of serenity to the image.

Cutting Tiles

Any shape can be cut from glass and ceramic with tile nippers. Hold the tile between the forefinger and thumb of one hand and, with the other, place the nippers on the edge of the tile. Squeeze gently, and the tile will break. Take care not to place the nippers all the way across the tile, or it might shatter. Tiles break along the line of the blades of the nippers, so make angled cuts, such as triangles, by placing the nippers diagonally across the tiles. You can draw lines on the tiles to guide you when shaping tiles, but use a pencil or a non-permanent marker so that you can rub off the ink.

Circles

Form circles by nibbling away fragments of material at the corners of a square tile until you have a smooth curve.

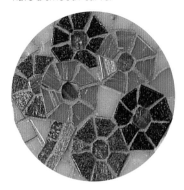

Triangles

To make a triangle, hold a tile by two opposing corners and nip the tile diagonally across the center. To make petals, cut a tile in half, then make diagonal cuts at each side.

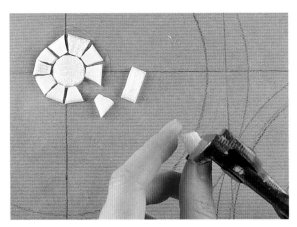

Fine Shapes

The simplest way to cut very fine pieces is to cut a tile in half, then in half again (creating a quarter tile), then cut the finer flaring shapes from these quarters. Cut back from the point, rather than from the widest side of the tile to the point. If you have difficulty, use the back of the tile nippers. This edge may be sharper.

Random Shapes

The way in which the tiles are laid will affect how much cutting you need to do. A "crazy laid" or non-directional background will need the fewest and easiest cuts. If you find it difficult to make shapes to fit a particular gap, mark the line of the cut on the tile with a pencil, then cut along it.

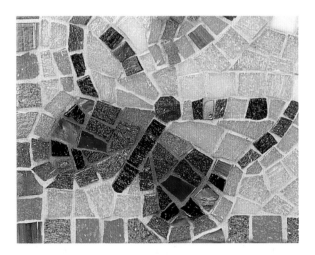

Following Curves

To create tiles that follow curves, first cut a tile in half. Then cut the diagonals from the half-cut tile by placing the nippers at a slight angle to the tile. As you move around a curve, think of the angles as slices of a pie. Work out where the center of your curve is in relation to the center of your imagined pie, and cut the diagonal line accordingly.

Thicker Materials

Marble, smalti, and some ceramic wall tiles are more difficult to cut and shape than vitreous glass tiles. Use long-handled tile nippers for greater leverage and place the nippers right across the tile in the line of the desired cut.

Styles of Laying

Whatever you are making in mosaic, the way you lay the tiles is a very important consideration, both in terms of the ease of execution and the finished appearance. If you are covering a considerable area in a single color, the laying technique (also known as coursing) assumes an even greater importance: the pattern of grout lines will be very dominant and should be carefully selected to create an effect that enhances the mosaic. The egg design below has been laid in six different ways to demonstrate this.

Directional lines

In illustrations 1, 2, and 3, the pieces are laid along directional lines. These continuous grout joints will appear stronger than the intermediate joints and will therefore emphasize the lines of laying.

1 The white mosaic tiles are laid in straight horizontal lines that make the egg look very flat. It would not be practical to lay this shape in vertical lines since the edge rows would have to be made of very small pieces, which are tricky to cut. In contrast, the black background is laid to the curve of the egg's outline to create a lively effect and emphasize the white shape. This method is used very effectively in the Peacock Slab on p. 155.

2 Here, a slightly curved line has been chosen for the white area, which gives the shape an almost 3-D quality. The same approach is used on the pear in the Kitchen Clock on p. 84. This effect is heightened by being set against a background that is laid in straight horizontal lines that create a much flatter appearance. Laying in parallel lines gives a calm and orderly effect and is usually the least obtrusive technique to use. It can also help emphasize lines of movement—for example of ripples in water, as in the Dragonfly Panel on p. 62.

3 Further emphasis can be added by using rectangular, rather than square, pieces. The long, thin shapes laid across the egg create a strong horizontal effect in contrast to the vertical laying of the background. This simple contrasting of vertical and horizontal elements is used to depict the buildings in the Cityscape on p. 95.

Non-directional lines

It is difficult to choose a line of laying for projects in which all the objects are equally important. If you don't want to emphasize one particular direction by using directional lines, choose a non-directional line that treats the items equally. Illustrations 4, 5, and 6 demonstrate techniques that create the effect of a uniform pattern of grout lines across the surface of the design using non-directional lines.

Below In this landscape made from vitreous glass, the lines of laying echo the shapes of the river, trees, and fields. Precise cutting is less important here than with ceramic tiles, but color is more of an issue.

4 In this example, whole tiles are laid along a grid of lines running in both directions. However, this main grid is occasionally interrupted by half and quarter tiles. These tiles help make the small cut pieces at the edge of the white shape less obvious. Still, cutting around the outline results in a much less elegant curve than in the other examples. It is a very unforgiving technique and works best with straight lines, as in the House Number project on p. 120.

5 This piece demonstrates a method of laying that uses random-sized pieces. It is flexible and can be applied to the most awkward of shapes, including 3-D designs such as the Mediterranean Planter on p. 133. Within the egg, there are some angled cuts that set the tiles off in different directions, while in the background all the pieces are roughly square or rectangular and laid parallel to the edges of the piece. The pattern of grout lines is thus busy and unpredictable, and provides a way of making the surface interesting while maintaining a very flat overall effect.

6 This example demonstrates the use of more orderly patterns that can be introduced to give large single-colored areas interest in a more structured and therefore calmer way. It can also be effective in a mosaic that uses a limited range of colors, as demonstrated with the Birdbath on p. 136.

Color

The mosaic palette is a fixed palette—you can't mix a mosaic color yourself. At the end of the nineteenth century in France, painters experimented with the principles of Michel-Eugène Chevreul (1786-1889), who studied the nature of color. These experiments—laying dabs of complementary color on the canvas that mix on the retina to produce a lively effect—are associated with impressionism and post-impressionism. The magnificent paintings that were produced at this time have a superficial visual relationship to mosaic, and mosaicists occasionally argue that the mosaicists of Byzantine churches and cathedrals understood these principles long before Chevreul "discovered" them. Mosaics made according to Chevreul's principles need distance to work effectively (the dome of a cathedral is ideal) or to be made at a very small scale. Both these requirements have their problems, which is why the beginner needs to understand both the limitations and the scope of a fixed palette of colors.

Issues of complementary colors, and "hot" and "cold" colors—in other words, the amount of red, yellow, or blue in a color—are meaningful only when one color is compared to another. On the other hand, the tone of a color is highly significant in mosaic-making. Tone is the degree of lightness or darkness of a color. Tiles of an entirely different color (or "hue") can be similar in tone, and it is critical to understand the perils this similarity can hold. If you make, for example, a green leaf on a blue background, and the tone of the leaf is the same as that of the background, the difference in hue will not be enough to make the leaf clearly distinguishable. Grout complicates the issue further.

Intensity is the degree of saturation or the brightness of a color. An intense color will stand out against colors of similar tone. Yellow vitreous glass tiles can be very bright, and dark blues are some of the most intense colors in the vitreous glass range. Purple and dark mauve vitreous glass tend to look gray from a distance.

HUE	**TONE**	**INTENSITY**
The basic color of the tiles, for example, green and blue.	*Whether they are dark, light, or in between.*	*Whether they are pure, bright, or muted.*

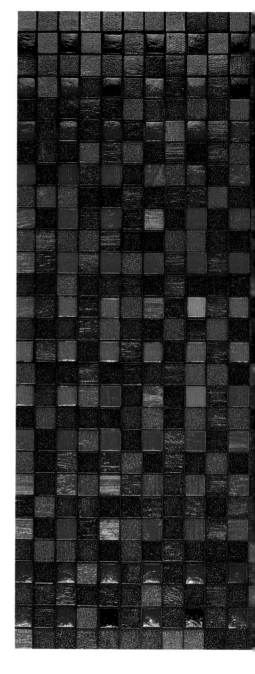

Above The different intensities of red and orange are shown in this panel. When bright tiles are separated by a grid of muted tiles, their pure color shines out.

Left It is always a good idea to make a sample selection of the tile colors you intend to use before starting work on a mosaic design. A single tile will look different when laid next to tiles of different hues, tones, and intensities.

Effect of grout color on design

Think of grout as you think of tone. White is light, gray is mid-tone, and charcoal gray is dark. With these three grout colors, you can mix any tone you might need. Mosaic generally looks least fractured and most integrated when you match the tone of the grout to the principal tone of the mosaic. On the other hand, if you have made a mistake and the color of all your tiles is tonally similar to the point of camouflage, you can make the mosaic clearer (at the expense of its looking fractured) by grouting with a contrasting color. A mosaic that depends on contrast (black and white for example) is generally best grouted a tone between the two, so both colors are broken up equally, rather than one dominating the other.

The difference grout color can make to tiles of a similar color is shown at right and below. These examples show the differing effects of white, gray, and charcoal gray grout. Notice the way the tonal relationships between tiles change according to the grout color.

Opinions differ on using colored grout, but unless you are very skillful or experienced, you should avoid using it.

White grout unites pale colors while its contrast of tone breaks up all the other colors.

Gray grout softens the effect of mid-tone colors.

Dark grout unites darker tones and contrasts with lighter ones.

Drawing and Tracing

When you want to design your own mosaics, or amend any of the designs given in this book, making a color sketch will help you choose which colored tiles to use and assess the quantities you will need. You can then be confident that your design will work before you embark on the process of creating it with mosaic tiles. Select colored pencils that match as nearly as possible your range of tiles. You can apply one color on top of another to adjust the shades to get a closer match. The sketches can be much smaller than the finished piece because what you are concentrating on is the overall composition and color balance. The drawings can be quite rough and quick so that you can experiment with a number of different options rather than producing a single careful drawing.

There are two basic techniques for enlarging designs, and for both it is easiest to work from a simple line drawing made by tracing over your color sketch. In the first method, draw a grid of squares over your line drawing, then draw a grid of the same number of squares (but of a bigger size) on the backing surface of the mosaic. For the Direct Method this will be the backing board itself. For the Indirect Method it will be a piece of brown paper cut to the same size as your board. (The size of each project is given in the "You Will Need" list.) Then, copy your line drawing, square by square, onto the larger surface. Charcoal is a good tool to use because it can be easily erased and adjusted. If you are using the Indirect Method, remember to reverse the drawing at this stage by turning over the gridded tracing.

The second technique is to enlarge your line drawing (or template, if you choose to use one) to the correct size on a photocopier and then trace it onto the backing surface following the instructions for templates below.

Using Templates

On pp. 158 to 169, you will find templates that you can copy to make mosaic designs from this book. To use the templates, begin by cutting a piece of tracing paper exactly to the size of the backing board you intend to use. Enlarge the template (or your line drawing) on a photocopier, then place the tracing paper over the template (or line drawing) and trace off the design using a soft pencil (ideally 2B or softer). Then follow the instructions for the Indirect or the Direct Method, depending on which of these techniques you intend to use.

For the Indirect Method

Turn the tracing paper over and place it (pencil side down) on top of a piece of brown paper of the same size. Follow the line with a hard pencil, pressing down firmly. This will transfer the original pencil line to the paper underneath, but with the image reversed. Go over the line on the brown paper with a permanent marker so that it does not rub off as you work.

For the Direct Method

Protect your work surface with scrap paper then turn the traced design pencil side down. Follow the line of the design on the back of the tracing paper using a soft pencil. (The original line will transfer onto the surface below, which is why you should protect it.) Then turn the tracing paper the right way up, place it on top of the board you intend to decorate, and trace the line again with a hard pencil. This will transfer the design the right way around onto the board below. Go over the transferred line with a permanent marker so that it does not rub off as you work.

Framing, Finishing, and Hanging

The edges of mosaics are always vulnerable to accidental damage, so pieces that are going to be frequently handled or moved, such as tabletops, should have a protective edging. Make tabletops on framed boards whenever possible. If you try to frame a completed mosaic, you may accidentally dislodge vulnerable edge pieces. If you want to paint the frame, do this before you start on the mosaic when the inside face of the frame is still accessible. This will ensure that there is a neat junction with the grout joint around the edge. Cover the perimeter of the board with strips of masking tape so that paint does not get on the surface: a layer of paint can interfere with adhesion. Grouting the mosaic may discolor the paintwork, but you can touch it up after you have completed fixing the piece. If a lot of repainting is necessary, first cover the mosaic with masking tape to protect the tiles.

The edges of unframed pieces can be strengthened by running a little extra adhesive around the sides. This also disguises the wooden backing material and gives the appearance of a cement slab. The adhesive can be painted to match the grout color when the adhesive is dry.

To hang wood-backed mosaics on a wall, screw two d-rings into the back of the board and thread picture wire between the rings. Mosaics made on tiles or tile-backer board can be glued to walls with a thin layer of cement-based adhesive. You might want to use a temporary support, such as a wooden batten, to take the weight of the mosaic while the adhesive dries.

Mosaic materials

Mosaics can be made from small pieces of almost any material, but glass, ceramic, and marble are intentionally in small sizes and are easy to cut and use. The choice of material depends both on the nature of the design and on the application. Most materials are suitable for small panels and wall mosaics, so the selection can be made on appearance alone. Materials for floors and paving slabs, however, must be hard wearing, and the range is therefore more limited.

Vitreous glass tiles

These factory-made tiles in glass paste (below) are probably the most popular form of mosaic and offer the widest range of colors. They are available in a wide range of beautiful colors and can be purchased on paper-faced sheets of single colors that are approximately 10 inches (30 cm) square and contain 225 tiles. The tiles can be easily removed from the paper by soaking the sheets in water for about 15 minutes. Spread the tiles out to dry before using them. Some suppliers sell tiles loose and in smaller quantities.

"Gemme" (right) are vitreous glass tiles striated with metallic ore that have a coppery or gold-streaked appearance.

ESTIMATING QUANTITIES If your design is very simple—for instance in black and white—you will be able to estimate quite accurately the required number of tiles, but for more complicated designs you just have to make a guess!

A common size for both vitreous glass and unglazed ceramic tiles is $3/4$ inch (20 mm) square, and one sheet (225 tiles) of these will cover about 1 foot (30 cm) square and will weigh $1\frac{1}{2}$ pounds (700 g). When cutting any tiles for a design, you should allow for about 20 percent waste.

You can buy a few sheets at a time, but colors sometimes vary from batch to batch. Therefore, if you plan to cover a large area with a single color, buy all your tiles at once.

Smalti

Smalti (left and above) is the traditional high-fired enameled glass material used by the Roman and Byzantine mosaicists that is still manufactured in and around Venice. It is made in large, irregular circles like omelets and cut up into slightly uneven rectangles that are sold by weight—each color is sold in a minimum quantity of 1 pound (½ kg). Alternatively, you can buy bags of mixed colors that are made up of the off-cuts from the edges of the "omelets." Smalti is intensely colored, which can make it difficult to use with subtlety. It works well when used in combination with marble.

Gold, silver, and metallic tiles

The finest metal-faced mosaic is made in Italy, where metal leaf is sandwiched between two layers of glass. For wall-quality gold, silver, and a range of other metals, the material is often backed with colored glass. Floor-quality material (*pavimento* gold or silver) is fixed on clear glass so you can look through to the metal finish below.

The reflective qualities can make these tiles difficult to use effectively on a small scale. Used on a large scale, they can look opulent, but at a fabulous price.

Less expensive metallic tiles are available. In these, the metal leaf is protected by a coat of painted primer only. They create a glittering effect, but are not recommended for use outdoors.

Stained glass

Opaque stained glass (below) is available in a variety of colors and interesting patterns and textures. It can be cut with a score-and-snap tile cutter and made into smaller glass tesserae. Clear glass can also be used and backed with metallic tape or metal leaf protected with a painted primer.

Mirror tiles

Mirror tiles are available on fabric-backed sheets that are useful for covering large areas. They are not easy to remove from their backing, but loose tiles can be purchased individually. Mirror tiles are available in thicknesses of ¹⁄₁₆ th and ⅛ th inches (2 mm and 3 mm), and in round shapes as well as squares.

Glazed ceramic

Most ordinary, glazed ceramic wall tiles can be cut down to use in mosaic designs, but avoid those with a beveled edge because they will look different from the others. Some glazed tiles are not frostproof and therefore are unsuitable for use outdoors. The harder the tile is to cut, the more likely it is to be frostproof. Very hard tiles can be cut with long-handled tile nippers, which give greater leverage. Try to use tiles of equal thickness in any design, as this will be easier to grout and will result in a smoother and more attractive surface.

Unglazed ceramic

This is one of the cheapest and most durable of mosaic materials and is produced in earthy, neutral tones. Ceramic tiles are available in either paper-faced sheets, like vitreous glass tiles, or on mesh-backed sheets. Peeling tiles off mesh can be time-consuming, so if you need loose tiles, choose paper-faced ones. Tiles are available in 1 inch (2.5 cm) and ¾ inch (20 mm) squares. A limited range of colors is also available in ¾ inch (20 mm) diameter circles.

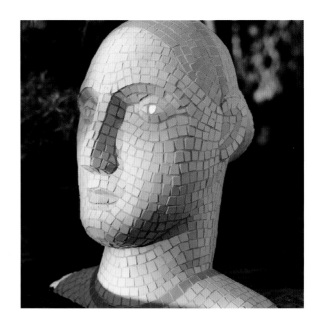

Ceramic tiles look the same on both sides, so if you make an inaccurate cut, you can often turn the tile over and start again. Ceramic is a material that draws attention to the way the tiles are laid, which can be a disadvantage if your cutting is not one hundred percent accurate!

Below Unglazed ceramic and vitreous glass tiles are used in this panel. These two materials are the same thickness and can be used together to exploit the variety of surface effect and intensity of color.

Right The use of a single color draws attention to the carefully controlled lines of laying. The head is made of unglazed ceramic on a cement and mesh base.

Marble

A marble tile has three faces: the polished, glassy face; the rough sawn face, and the riven (or broken) internal face. The internal color of marble is difficult to determine by looking at the sawn face because saw marks leave the cubes with a whitish finish. The riven face exposes the natural color of the marble and has a textured finish. The polished face shows the natural color, but has a smooth surface. Each of these finishes has its uses: polished or sawn face material is best for paving, and the uneven riven marble is more suitable for walls. The differences between them are marked when the material is dry. Wetting them makes them all look similar by heightening the intensity of color.

Part of the process of cutting cubes (the name given to small marble mosaic tiles) involves cutting larger sheets into rods (right). Cubes are then cut from these long, thin pieces. Marble cubes are available in single colors on a webbed backing in sheets approximately 1 foot (30 cm) square. This backing is designed to be impossible to remove, so if you intend to use the cubes loose, it is important to buy them loose. You can cut cubes in half yourself with tile nippers, but wear goggles to protect your eyes from flying debris.

Marble is an expensive material, but masons' yards and tile stores often have off-cuts that they will sell at a discount. Some kinds of marble are suitable for exterior use, others are not. If in doubt, ask your mason or supplier for advice. It is frustrating to put an enormous amount of effort into making a mosaic only to have it change color or fall apart because you have chosen the wrong marble.

Other materials

Any material that naturally comes in small pieces can be used in mosaic: shells, marbles, pebbles, metal nuts, beads, buttons, and so on. Equally suitable is any material that can be cut or broken easily, such as colored glass, mirror glass, and pottery.

Above This fish is made using the riven face of the marble, which has a lively, irregular surface and reveals the crystalline composition of the natural stone.

Left Different materials can be combined if they are chosen with care. Here, the pebbles, shells, marbles, and beads are all of a similar size and shape, giving a sense of order as well as variety.

Bases

Mosaic can be fixed to a variety of bases as long as the correct adhesive is used and the background is stiff and stable. Wood supports, such as plywood, are the most convenient bases to use, but for more permanent installations mosaic designs can be stuck directly to walls and floors. The Indirect Method (see p. 38) is particularly suitable for these applications, since it allows the mosaic to be made on a table before being fixed in position.

Boards

If you are making a wall panel or tabletop for indoor use, you can use any kind of wood or plywood, but M.D.F. (medium density fiber board) is particularly suitable because it is very stable and will not warp or move with atmospheric changes. Very thin boards—3/8 inch (9 mm) thick—can be used as bases for mosaics of up to 16 inches (40 cm) square. Larger mosaics need thicker boards to ensure stiffness. For pieces over 1 yard (1 m) square, be sure to use a 1/2 inch (12 mm) board with cross-bracing at the back to reduce the weight of the finished piece. Before starting a

mosaic this size that you intend to hang on a wall, attach a batten to the back of the board. Hanging brackets can be screwed to this when you have finished the piece.

If you are making a mosaic piece that is intended for outdoor use, you should use exterior-grade plywood, exterior M.D.F. (which is more stable than ply), or marine ply, which can even withstand salt water. Remember that the fixings for an outdoor piece must all be rust-proof—made of brass, stainless steel, or galvanized. The edges of panels are vulnerable to knocks, so glue or pin a frame of beading to the sides of plywood and M.D.F. boards. You can also use other framing materials such as copper strip nailed in place with copper pins, or aluminum or brass corner angles screwed into the back of the board. If the piece is to be left unframed, the edges should be protected with extra adhesive around the perimeter. (See p. 22 for more on Framing, Finishing, and Hanging.)

Walls

Beginners should make their mosaics on boards. However, more advanced mosaicists may wish to fix a mosaic directly onto a wall. If you want to do this, you must bear in mind certain guidelines. If you plan to fix a mosaic onto existing plaster, first seal the wall with a preparatory primer. Sand-and-cement render (see p. 31) is a good backing for mosaic and essential in wet areas and outdoors. Cement-based adhesives (see p. 30) will stick to painted surfaces, but the bond between the render and the paint must be sound and all flaking areas removed. If you use a thin-bed adhesive, the surface must be flat because any bumps and hollows will show up in the finished mosaic. Rub off lumps with a grinding stone and fill hollows with cement-based adhesive.

Floors

A concrete floor with a layer of sand and cement (screed) provides a good backing surface for a mosaic floor, but be sure to note that flatness is even more crucial on floors than on walls. Allow new screed floors to dry out completely before covering them with mosaic. Existing surfaces should be sound, dry, and clean. Prepare wood floorboards before using them as a base by covering them in ¾ inch (20 mm) plywood screwed down at 9 inch (23 cm) intervals. Cover bathroom and kitchen floors in marine ply that will stand up to damp conditions.

Terra-cotta and concrete

Terra-cotta planters and concrete paving slabs can be used as mosaic backings. Prime these porous surfaces first with washable P.V.A. (see p. 30) diluted 50:50 with water and allow them to dry. You can then fix mosaic tiles to the surface with a cement-based adhesive using the Direct or Indirect Method. (See pp. 34 to 41 for these methods.)

Adhesives and grout

The choice of adhesive depends on the material being used, the base to which it is stuck, and whether the mosaic is for indoor or outdoor use.

Polyvinyl acetate (P.V.A.)

P.V.A. is a white liquid glue that comes in various degrees of permanence. For sticking mosaic materials to paper in the Indirect Method (see p. 38), you will need washable P.V.A. that dissolves when wet. Dilute the glue 50:50 with water before brushing it onto the paper.

Non-washable P.V.A. and E.V.A. (ethylene acetate) are used in the Direct Method (see p. 34) and are suitable for fixing flat-backed materials such as ceramic tiles to wood or M.D.F. bases. P.V.A. is suitable for dry areas, while E.V.A. should be used for wet areas. However, neither should be used for external locations.

If you're not sure what kind of P.V.A. you have, stick down one or two tiles on paper, leave them to dry, then try to soak them off.

Silicone glue

This is a thick jelly-like glue that comes in various colors, including translucent, and is available in most hardware stores. It is generally sold in cartridges for mastic guns or in small tubes. Silicone sealant is recommended for gluing glass, and clear silicone is available at specialist glaziers. Its translucence and flexibility make it especially suitable for sticking glass to glass. It can be messy to use. Any excess silicone should be scrubbed off with a brush and water before it dries because it is very difficult to remove afterward. The glue is water-resistant so the materials you are gluing down must be dry. Silicone skins over very quickly when exposed to the air, so apply it to the back of each tile rather than spreading it over the surface to be decorated.

Cement-based adhesives

These are proprietary tiling adhesives based on the traditional mixture of sand and cement, but enhanced with modern chemical additives. Some products are suitable only for interior use, so study the manufacturer's instructions carefully. Rapid-setting adhesives can be used with the Indirect Method (see p. 38), but slow-setting adhesives are better for the Direct Method (see p. 34) because they give a longer working time.

When sticking to boards for interior use, make sure the adhesive contains a flexible additive that will allow for the natural movement in the wood.

In exterior locations, boards will move even more, so you should use a highly flexible adhesive that includes latex. Latex improves the flexibility and adhesion of the adhesive and should be used if the mosaic will be subject to special strains such as handling, vibration, or variations in temperature. It is also recommended for use in wet areas.

Sand and cement

A mixture of sand and cement is the traditional material for fixing mosaic. It is still widely used for fixing floors where a level surface is necessary. The sand and cement mixture is laid in a bed up to 1¼ inch (3 cm) thick. The mosaic is then beaten down into it, thus evening out any minor irregularities in either the sub-base or the mosaic. Fixing mosaic in this way is an art; if you are a beginner, attend a specialized course or choose another method!

Cement-based grout

Grout is a weak mix of sand and cement—in other words, it is mostly sand—that is used to fill the joints between tiles and to allow movement without cracking. Grout is available ready-mixed and in powder, which you mix with water. Because it is a very fine powder, water should be added gradually until a workable paste is formed. Grout is available from hardware stores in a range of colors. Always bear in mind the tone of the grout, even if the color matches that of the mosaic tiles. Different tones of gray can also make a great difference to the finished appearance and can be achieved by mixing light gray and black grout. (See p. 19 for more about the effects of grout color.)

Right Grout color radically changes the look of a finished mosaic, as shown by these samples grouted in white and black.

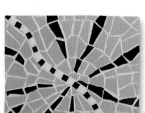

Grouting

Grouting the joints of a mosaic gives it a uniform surface that can be washed down, which is essential in areas that need to be kept clean, such as kitchens and bathrooms. Any kind of tiling grout can be used, although manufacturers often recommend using a finer grout for narrow joints. Always wear rubber gloves (not latex gloves, which are not strong enough) when grouting. Grout contains cement, which is not good for the skin.

In the Direct Method (see p. 34), grout is applied in a single process when the adhesive is completely dry. The surface of the mosaic is covered in the wet grout mixture, then wiped off immediately, leaving the grout in the joints. In the Indirect Method (see p. 38) the mosaic is grouted in two stages. The first stage is called pre-grouting: the mosaic is grouted from the back when it is still stuck to the paper. The backs of the tiles are sponged clean, leaving the grout to fill the joints. This stops the adhesive from coming up between the joints and also improves the adhesion of the mosaic to the backing material. When the paper has been peeled away, the excess grout on the face of the mosaic is sponged off while it is still wet and before it can harden into an uneven surface. The second stage—re-grouting—can be left until the adhesive is dry. Re-grouting fills the tiny holes left by air pockets and excess glue. This is easiest to do if you wet the mosaic first, because it allows the grout to spread more easily over the surface and to stick to the existing grout in the joints. Again, the grout must be sponged off immediately so that it doesn't dry on the face of the tiles. If you are left with a residue of grout on the surface of the mosaic, clean it with a mortar cleaner available at builders' merchants.

Purely decorative mosaics, such as those made of uneven materials such as smalti and riven marble, don't have to be grouted. The absence of grout can intensify colors and give the mosaic a more textured surface.

Tools

Whatever mosaic you plan to make, you will need tile nippers and a tool for applying adhesive and grout. If you intend to use the Direct Method (see p. 34), you will need an adhesive spreader for cement-based adhesive or a small brush to spread P.V.A., depending on the surface you plan to cover. A grout spreader and a decorator's sponge will make the grouting process easier and will improve the finished product. If you plan to make a mosaic using the Indirect Method (see p. 38), you will need a notched trowel for spreading the adhesive.

1. Tile nippers These are essential tools for cutting and shaping small pieces of all mosaic materials. To cut brittle materials, such as glass and ceramic, place the nippers on the edge of the tile—not all the way across, or the tile might shatter. When cutting thicker materials, such as marble and smalti, place the nippers across the piece in the line of the desired cut. Accurate cutting takes some practice, but remember that pieces that come out the wrong shape are bound to fit beautifully somewhere else in your mosaic. Tile nippers with long handles are also available. These provide greater leverage, which make them ideal for cutting harder materials.

2. Double-wheeled tile nippers have two circular blades that cut very accurately and are ideal for cutting sheet glass and smalti.

3. Glass cutter Ordinary glass cutters with a sharp, scoring wheel are available at hardware stores and are used for scoring a line in stained and mirrored glass. The scored glass can then be snapped by the snapper on a tile cutter or by hand by holding the glass close to the score line with pliers and snapping it with finger and thumb on the other side of the line. Glass cutters can also be used to score gold and silver tiles to create more accurate cuts.

4. Tile cutter This tool is also known as a score-and-snap cutter. It has a scoring wheel that runs along the line of the cut and a snapper to break the tile along the scored line. Available at all tile stores, tile cutters are useful for cutting large tiles (such as ceramic wall tiles) into manageable pieces.

5. A plastic comb and blade is used for grouting and applying adhesive to small areas.

6. A rubber-blade squeegee is used to grout medium-sized pieces, such as tabletops.

7. Flat-bed squeegees are used for grouting large jobs, such as pavements and murals.

8. The ⅛ inch (3 mm) notched trowel is the standard mosaicist's tool for applying thin-bed cement-based adhesive to all types of backings.

9. A V-notched trowel is useful for fixing mosaics that use very small pieces because the shape of the teeth allows for a very fine covering of adhesive.

10. A plasterer's small tool is a metal modeling tool—with one pointed and one square end—that is invaluable for applying adhesive to both flat and curved surfaces when using the Direct Method (see p. 34).

NOTE Wear safety goggles and a mask whenever you are cutting tiles. Use a brush to sweep up dust and shards of glass regularly. Never use your hands, since you risk cutting yourself.

Basic methods

The main fixing methods described here are easy to follow, and practice is the best way to iron out any difficulties you may experience and gain confidence. Before embarking on a large project, make a small sample using the appropriate technique. This will give you a feel of the method and a preview of how the finished mosaic will look. This is particularly helpful when it comes to choosing the best grout color or tone. Which method you use to make your mosaic is largely a matter of personal choice.

The Direct Method

The Direct Method describes the technique of sticking mosaic pieces directly to the backing material. It is a straightforward process, but it requires some careful planning because it is difficult to make alterations once you have stuck down the pieces. It is the essential technique for 3-D work, but can also be used on flat surfaces. This technique is also useful when the material you are using has a different appearance on the front and back faces. An example of this is glazed ceramic, such as the wall tiles used in the Sunburst Mirror Frame.

Direct onto a flat surface—Sunburst Mirror Frame

YOU WILL NEED:

- Masking tape
- 16 inch (40 cm) diameter framed board
- Paint and paintbrush
- Pencil
- Ruler
- Mirror
- Mirror glue
- Tile cutter
- Tile nippers
- Cloth
- Hammer
- Non-washable P.V.A. glue and brush to apply it
- White grout
- Rubber gloves
- Sponge
- Lint-free cloth

MATERIALS

- Glazed ceramic wall tiles, gold tiles, ceramic plate

For this frame, the mosaic tiles are glued directly onto the base board, right side up. When making a mosaic mirror frame, note that the area to be tiled must be wide enough to allow for an interesting pattern, but not so wide that it makes the mirror look tiny in the middle. As a general rule, the diameter of the mirror should be larger than the width of the surrounding area. This project uses a framed board, the raised edge of which helps protect the outer pieces of mosaic. If you don't have a framed board, use a circle of M.D.F. and paint the edges white to match the grout.

1 Mask the board and paint the edges of the frame. Leave to dry. With a pencil and ruler, draw radiating lines from the center of the frame to its edge to act as a guide for positioning the tiles. Squeeze out a couple of lines of mirror glue onto the back of the mirror. Place the mirror on the board and swivel it so that the glue is thoroughly dispersed.

2 To cut the wall tiles into strips, score a line on the tiles with a tile cutter. Then, place the tile cutter over the score mark and snap. To make the strips fit around the circle, taper them slightly at one end by angling the scored line.

3 Shape the gold tiles into rounds by gradually "nibbling" away the corners with the tile nippers. Cover the plate with a cloth to prevent plate shards from flying everywhere, then smash the plate into small pieces with a hammer. (Cups and mugs are not recommended for this kind of project because they have rounded sides.)

4 Fix the mosaic pieces to the board with a thick layer of P.V.A. glue, applying the glue to the board (not the tiles). Cut more tiles to fit the frame as you need them. Try to keep a consistent gap between the different elements.

5 Mix up the grout and spread it over the surface of the tiles, working it up to the edge of the mirror. Use a gloved hand to push the grout into the joints between the tiles. Rub off the excess with your fingers as you go. Try to avoid getting grout on the mirror as it can scratch. (You can mask the mirror to protect it if you wish. See p. 22 for instructions.)

6 Clean off the grout immediately with a sponge soaked in clean water and wrung out until just damp. Keeping the sponge as flat as possible, move it across the mosaic in one big sweep, then turn the sponge. (Going over the tiles with a dirty sponge smears them with grout.) This way you ensure the surface gets clean with the minimum of effort. When you have used all six sides of the sponge, wash it out in a bucket, then repeat until the mosaic surface is clean. Leave the mosaic to dry for one hour, then buff it up with a dry lint-free cloth.

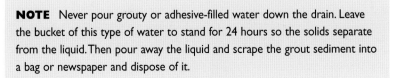

NOTE Never pour grouty or adhesive-filled water down the drain. Leave the bucket of this type of water to stand for 24 hours so the solids separate from the liquid. Then pour away the liquid and scrape the grout sediment into a bag or newspaper and dispose of it.

Direct onto a 3-D surface—Striped Pot

The key to success when applying mosaic tiles to a 3-D object is to use an adhesive that is appropriate for both the background on which you are working and the location of the finished piece. (See p. 30.) This method is demonstrated on a terra-cotta pot, which is intended for outdoor use. The straight sides of this pot provide the perfect surface for a simple design of vertical stripes. Because terra-cotta is porous, you should first seal the pot by applying a 50:50 solution of washable P.V.A. glue and water and leaving it to dry. This will prevent the cement-based adhesive from drying out too quickly.

When choosing a 3-D object to cover in mosaic, bear in mind that some of the properties of mosaic can cause problems. For example, when marble cubes are fixed and grouted, they are very heavy. Another consideration is that mosaic is not very pleasant to touch and is unsuitable for things that should be smooth and tactile, such as handrails and door handles. Mosaic can also be vulnerable to knocks and general handling, so any object that has exposed mosaic edges should be treated with care.

YOU WILL NEED:

- Terra-cotta pot
- Brown paper
- Pencil
- Scissors
- Tile nippers
- Plasterer's small tool
- Cement-based adhesive
- Rubber gloves
- Grout
- Sponge
- Lint-free cloth

MATERIALS

- Vitreous glass tiles

1 First, make a paper template so that you can work out your design on a flat surface. Measure the height of the pot and cut out a long strip of paper of that width. Hold this up to the pot and wrap it around, allowing at least ¼ inch (5mm) overlap to account for the thickness of the mosaic and the adhesive bed. You can also use the edge of the paper to sketch a vertical line down the side of the pot if you wish.

2 With the tile nippers, begin cutting the tiles in half. Lay them out on the paper template, working out sequences of colors and interlocking patterns. Adjust the spacing to avoid a row of unattractive cuts either at the bottom of the pot or where the pattern meets up at the back.

3 Stick the tiles to the surface of the pot using a cement-based adhesive mixed to a stiff paste. Apply it with the plasterer's small tool. The adhesive will begin to skin over after 15 minutes, so apply only a small patch at a time. Try to avoid turning the pot, because you can easily knock off tiles that you have just stuck down. Either place the piece on top of a high stool or table and move around it yourself, or place it on a board that can be turned, such as a Lazy Susan.

4 When all the tiles are stuck on and the adhesive is completely dry, grout the mosaic. Put on the rubber gloves, then grout the mosaic by hand. Sponge off excess grout with the clean face of a sponge wiped diagonally across the line of the joints. When you have used all six sides of the sponge, wash it out in a bucket. Repeat until the surface is clean. Leave the mosaic to dry, then buff it up with a dry lint-free cloth.

The Indirect Method

The Indirect Method is the technique of making mosaics in reverse on paper before fixing them to the backing material, and finally removing the paper from the face—the front—of the finished piece. Although it involves an extra stage in the process, it has distinct advantages in some situations. Because all the tiles are fixed at once, it is easy to achieve a flat surface, which is desirable for tabletops and floors. This technique is widely used by professional mosaicists because it allows large projects to be made up in the workshop and transported to the site for assembly.

Horse Tile

The Indirect Method allows you to take your time with a piece without worrying that the adhesive will dry out before you have made your design decisions. Another advantage is that you can make small alterations to your design by peeling mosaic tiles from the backing paper and replacing them before the mosaic is grouted. The best paper to use for the Indirect Method is strong, brown craft paper that won't disintegrate while you're working and will peel off in one piece. It has a rough and a shiny side; tiles should be stuck to the rough side only.

A decorated tile like this one can be used as a pot stand if you glue felt to the base to prevent it from scratching the surface of your table. Alternatively, you can fix decorated tiles to a wall with tiling adhesive or use tiles as decorative panels in a garden or as a backsplash behind a sink in your kitchen or bathroom.

1 Cut a piece of brown paper to fit the floor tile you intend to mosaic. With the charcoal stick, sketch your design on the rough (not shiny) side of the paper. Charcoal is ideal because it is easy to erase. Select your tiles.

YOU WILL NEED:

- Scissors
- Brown paper
- Ceramic floor tile
- Charcoal stick
- Tile nippers
- Washable P.V.A. glue diluted 50:50 with water
- Brush
- Grout
- Rubber gloves
- Sponge
- Cement-based adhesive
- 1/8 inch (3 mm) notched trowel
- Small board
- Hammer
- Grouting squeegee

MATERIALS

- Vitreous glass tiles

2 With the tile nippers, cut the tiles into quarters by cutting them in half, then in half again. Brush the P.V.A. glue onto the paper and stick the tiles to it, flat side down and with the ridged backs facing you. Make sure you leave a consistent gap between them. Work in small sections, creating the main figures first and filling in the background last. Nip the tiles into shapes that fit the design. Leave to dry for one hour.

3 Cover your work surface with brown paper. Pre-grout the mosaic using your gloved hand to work the grout between the tiles. Filling the gaps between the tiles with grout prevents the adhesive (applied in Step 5) from squeezing up between the joints. It also helps the adhesive to bond.

4 Clean the mosaic with a damp sponge. Clean in a series of single sweeps, and at the end of each sweep, turn the sponge. When all six sides of the sponge have been used, clean it and squeeze until dry. Continue until grout is left only in the joints. Be careful not to flood the mosaic with water, since this will dissolve the glue too quickly and the tiles will fall off.

5 With the notched trowel, spread cement-based adhesive evenly over the unglazed side of the floor tile. You are applying the adhesive properly if you hear a scraping sound as you pull the trowel across the tile. Pick up the pre-grouted mosaic by diagonally opposed corners and lay it face down on the adhesive bed. Press down firmly over the whole surface. To be sure that all the mosaic pieces are properly bedded, place a small board over the mosaic and tap lightly with a hammer to expel pockets of air that can prevent proper bonding.

6 Dampen the backing paper with a sponge, keeping the paper wet for about ten minutes. As soon as all the paper is dark in color (the dark color tells you it is damp), begin to peel the paper off from one corner of the front of the mosaic. If tiles are still stuck to the paper, replace it and wait a little longer for the glue to dissolve. When the paper comes off easily, peel it back flat on itself. Avoid pulling upward, since this will lift the tiles away from the adhesive bed. When you reach halfway, lay the paper back down and peel from the other side. If you keep peeling up to the opposite edge, the tiles are very likely to come up. If this happens, do not panic. All you need do is place a dot of adhesive on the tile, ensure the hole it came from is empty, and replace it. When the paper has been completely removed, spread a little adhesive around the edge of the mosaic with a gloved hand to protect the perimeter pieces.

7 Before the grout dries on the front of the mosaic, gently clean it off with a damp sponge. When the adhesive is dry, the piece can be re-grouted with fresh grout. (This will spread more easily if you dampen the face of the mosaic beforehand.) Spread the grout over the mosaic with a grouting squeegee. Don't forget the edges of the tile. Work the grout in well, then clean the surface with a squeezed-out sponge and leave to dry for at least an hour. Rub off any residual grout with a dry lint-free cloth.

Casting

This technique lets you make individual mosaic paving slabs that you can combine into a garden path or use as a decorative feature in a lawn or an area of gravel. Working with sand and cement is not a precise science, so experiment with the proportions and keep a note of the most successful mixtures for future reference. As an alternative, you can fix vitreous glass tiles or marble cubes to ready-made slabs. However, if you need a special size or thickness to match existing paving, make your own following this method. Remember that sand and cement are heavy and cast slabs are difficult to handle.

YOU WILL NEED:

- Scissors
- Brown paper
- Washable P.V.A. glue diluted 50:50 with water
- Brush
- Long-handled tile nippers
- Casting frame, inner dimensions 1 foot (30 cm) square
- Cloth
- Petroleum jelly
- 2 buckets (1 for water, 1 for sand and cement)
- Rubber gloves
- Sand
- Cement

- Grouting squeegee
- Sponge
- Grout
- Wire mesh, 1 foot (30 cm) square
- Wire cutters
- Mixing tool (flat-ended trowel or wide wallpaper scraper)
- Flat-bed squeegee
- Screwdriver
- Board to turn over mosaic

MATERIALS

- Approximately 4 pounds (2 kg) marble cubes, 1/2 inch (12 mm) thick

NOTE A mixture of sand and cement on a wall is called a render; a mixture used on the floor is referred to as a screed. Many people make the mistake of calling this mixture cement, which is the name of the powder, or concrete, which is a very strong and stable mixture of sand, cement, and an aggregate such as pebbles.

1 Create your mosaic design following Steps 1 and 2 of the Indirect Method on p. 38. With a cloth, grease the inside of the casting frame with petroleum jelly to prevent sand and cement from sticking to the frame. Place your dry, completed mosaic in the frame, paper side down.

2 To make a cement slurry, mix four parts sand and one part cement in a bucket. Add water (the task is heavier and more laborious once the materials are wet). It is impossible to give precise instructions about how much water to add, because the quantity depends on how wet your sand is, but the slurry should not be running with water, or sloppy. Mix again. If you put in too much water, simply add the same proportions of dry sand and cement. The ideal consistency could be described as creamy if it were not so granular. Wearing rubber gloves, pre-grout the mosaic using the grouting squeegee to work the slurry into the joints. If this is the first time you have used marble, you may be surprised by how much grout you need. Because it is thicker than vitreous glass or ceramic tiles, marble needs a much greater quantity of grout.

3 Scrape off as much excess slurry as possible with the squeegee, then soak the sponge in water and squeeze it out until it is as dry as possible. Draw the sponge across the surface of the mosaic in one sweep, turn to a clean side of the sponge and repeat. When you have used all six sides of the sponge, rinse it out and repeat until the mosaic is completely clean.

4 Try to judge how much sand and cement will fill the frame, and make this much of a mixture of three parts sand to one part cement. Add just enough water to make this workable (not wet). Spread a layer of this over the mosaic, to about halfway up the frame. Add the square of wire mesh, then fill the frame to the top with the remaining sand and cement. (The mesh strengthens the sand and cement.) Firmly push down the mixture with a flat-bed squeegee, making sure all the corners of the frame are filled and the surface is even. Place the frame in a plastic bag for 24 hours. This allows the slab to begin the process of curing or setting and the plastic bag stops it from happening too fast and cracking.

5 After two to four days the slab should have set hard enough for you to handle it. Timing is crucial here: if you remove the slab from the frame too early, or are not sufficiently careful, you risk cracking it. If, on the other hand, you leave the slab for a week or so you may have trouble removing the backing paper. This is not generally a problem with glass or ceramic, but can be a problem with marble, particularly unpolished marble, because the surface is absorbent and takes up the glue (and the paper). Unscrew the sides of the casting frame and remove them. Place a small board on top of the mosaic—now sandwiched between the board and the bottom of the casting frame—and carefully turn it over.

6 If the paper on the face of the mosaic has dried out, wet it and leave it for at least ten minutes before peeling. Next, re-grout the face of the mosaic, sponge it off, and leave it for another week in a plastic bag until it has set solid. Buff up the mosaic, and lay the completed slab in your garden.

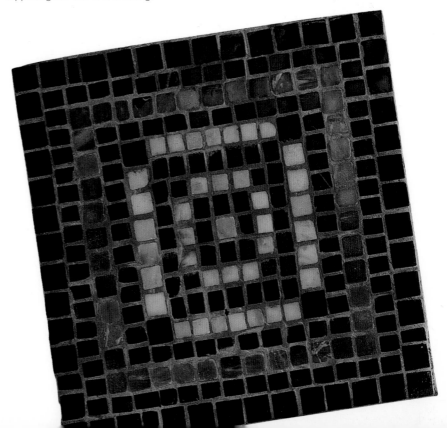

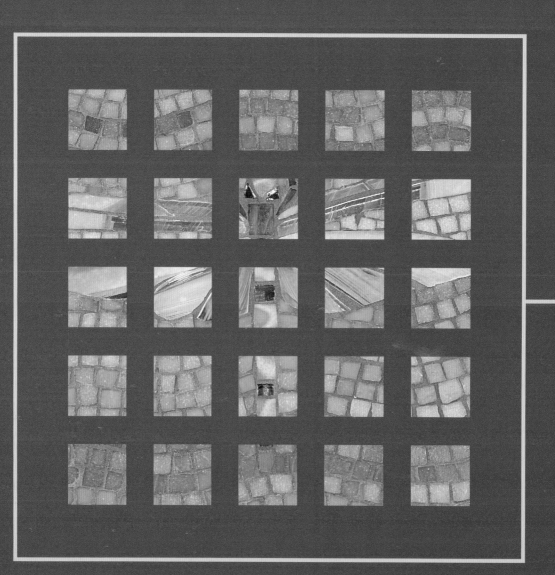

indoor projects

Bird Mirror Frame

This mirror frame is inspired by simple embroidery designs. It is made up of squares and triangles, laid on a regular grid, and is an easy project suitable for beginners. The geometric design is emphasized by the use of two different whites and two different blues that maintain a regular checkerboard pattern across the whole piece. This also gives a flickering and lively quality to the surface and a brighter intensity to the blues.

The piece is grouted in a gray grout, an intermediate tone that breaks up the blues and whites equally. Choosing the grout color can be difficult even for such a simple design. A white grout would unite the background and fracture the birds, while a dark grout would do the opposite. Sometimes this imbalance can be attractive and, because this is a symmetrical design, it would not throw the whole piece out of balance. However, the gray grout unites the piece into a satisfying whole. Many simple designs along the same lines can be created by playing around with graph paper, but try to limit the range of colors and make sure they contrast strongly with each other.

YOU WILL NEED:

- Square mirror
- Graph paper
- Blue pencils
- Template from p. 158 (optional)
- Board, 16 x 16 inches (40 x 40 cm)
- Ruler
- Pencil
- Tile nippers
- Non-washable P.V.A. glue and brush to apply it
- Mirror glue
- Masking tape
- Brown paper
- Rubber gloves
- Gray grout
- Grout spreader
- Sponge
- Lint-free cloth

MATERIALS

- Vitreous glass tiles (approximately 50 in two different whites; 75 in two different blues)

1 **Outline the mirror** on the graph paper and count the number of tiles that will fit around it, allowing for at least 1/16th inch (1.5 mm) joints between the tiles. Sketch your design with blue pencils. (Alternatively, use the template provided on p. 158.)

2 **Create a grid** on the board using a ruler and pencil, leaving a blank square where the mirror will go. The grid does not have to be exactly accurate, but will serve as a guide for setting the tiles.

3 **Referring to the graph paper drawing,** mark the blue areas with hatched pencil on the board. Cut the vitreous glass tiles into quarters with tile nippers, trying to keep them as square as possible. Apply P.V.A. glue to the border lines and stick down blue tiles of alternating shades.

4 **Continue sticking,** working on the pattern and background at the same time. Cut some of the tiles into triangles by placing the nippers diagonally across the edge of the tiles and squeezing. Try using the back of the nippers, which may be sharper and so give a better angle of cut.

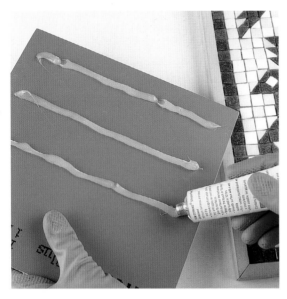

5 **When all the tiles are stuck down**, put on the rubber gloves and fix the mirror to the center of the board. Apply lines of mirror glue to the back of the mirror and carefully press it down into position.

6 **Before grouting,** cover the mirror with brown paper to ensure that it does not get scratched. Cut the paper smaller than the mirror and stick the masking tape on the exact edge of the mirror without overlapping the joint between the mirror and the surrounding tiles. Work grout into all the joints with the small grout spreader.

7 **Remove the excess** grout immediately by wiping the mosaic with the clean face of a damp sponge. Remove the paper and tape from the mirror. When the grout is dry, buff up the mosaic with a dry lint-free cloth.

Round Mirror Frame

A mosaic design is most effective when it responds to the fixed elements you have to work with—in this case, the circular shape of the frame. Repetition also makes a design visually pleasing. This mosaic takes these principles as a starting point and uses repeated and interrupted circles in a variety of sizes. As you can see, the repetition here is the circular board, the circular mirror, and the circular mounds of blossoms that contain circular flowers with round centers.

These repetitions would be tedious were it not for the use of asymmetry, both of form and color, that brings a surprise to what might otherwise be a predictable design. If you decide to create your own design, make sure you follow these guidelines.

YOU WILL NEED:

- Template from p. 159
- Soft pencil (2B or softer)
- Tracing paper
- Permanent marker
- 16 inch (40 cm) diameter framed board
- Paint, brush, and masking tape for frame
- Circular mirror
- Mirror glue
- Latex gloves
- Tile nippers
- Non-washable P.V.A. glue and brush to apply it
- Rubber gloves
- Scissors
- Gray grout
- Sponge
- Grouting squeegee
- Lint-free cloth

MATERIALS

- Vitreous glass tiles including silver tiles (used for their turquoise backs)

1 **Mask the board** and paint the edge of the mirror frame. When dry, remove the masking tape. Enlarge the template on a photocopier, and trace the pattern onto the framed board with a soft pencil. (See Drawing and Tracing, p. 20.) Go over the pencil lines on the board with a permanent marker.

2 **Fix the mirror to the board.** Protect your hands with latex gloves, then squeeze lines of mirror glue onto the back of the mirror. Place it on the board, mirror side up. Swivel the mirror so the glue is thoroughly dispersed. Cover the mirror with the center of the tracing paper from Step 1 to protect it from scratches.

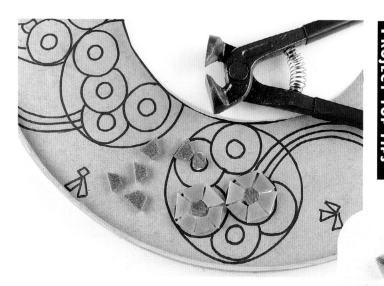

PROJECT TOP TIPS

Always glue the mirror in position before making the mosaic. It might seem logical to complete the mosaic first, but this can cause problems. If you accidentally lay tiles over the guidelines, the mirror may no longer fit, and you might have to remove tiles to make space for it.

3 **Start by shaping** the center of the flowers. To form a circle, cut a tile into quarters, then "nibble" off the corners. Make the surrounding petals from half tiles with a diagonal cut at each side. You can draw lines on the tiles to guide you (see Cutting Tiles p. 14), but use a non-permanent marker so that you can rub off the ink.

4 **The petals radiate** around the flower centers like slices of a pie, each cut leading to the center. You can make up your own rule—all the cuts could be straight-sided on the right and flare to the left, for example—but once you have decided what the rule is, stick to it.

5 **Using tones of blue** and pale lavender gives the piece a livelier effect than using flat, single colors would do. The brown branches that join the blossoms change tone from lighter to slightly darker against the lighter background color.

6 **What seemed unbalanced** in the line drawing in Step 1 (a cluster of blossoms at the top and bottom of the drawing and an empty space on the left-hand side) is evened out by bright color. The two lighter colored groups balance the pink and orange blossoms. The design needed some orange as a balance on the left-hand side, but not so much that the orange circle slips off the edge of the frame.

7 **Lay the background** fairly haphazardly, and don't strictly outline every form—this is a convention that can be static and tedious. A freer placement of tiles lends an energy to the background that matches that of the little shimmery insects.

8 **Insert the turquoise insects** where the rows of tiles make it easiest for you to do so. (The turquoise tile is actually the back of a silver tile.) Straining for an effect never looks as good as something that comes naturally when you are working.

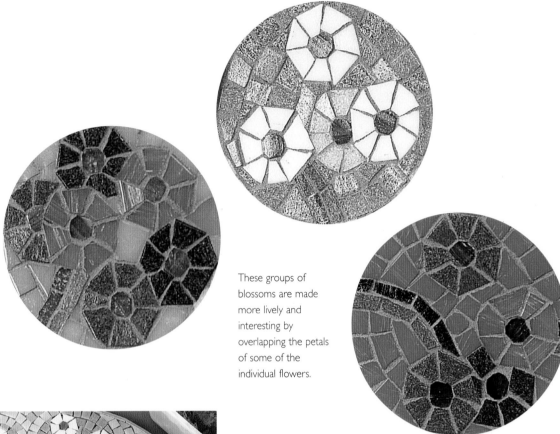

These groups of blossoms are made more lively and interesting by overlapping the petals of some of the individual flowers.

9 **When the entire design** is complete and dry, grout the mosaic with the grouting squeegee. Make sure you fill the joint between the mirror and the surrounding mosaic tiles.

10 **Sponge off the grout** using the clean face of a damp sponge. Remove the tracing paper on the mirror. When the grout is dry, buff up the mosaic with a dry lint-free cloth.

Butterfly Tile

This small and fairly simple project teaches the new mosaicist something about the lines of laying or coursing (the way the mosaic background is laid around an image), and demonstrates the effect of grout color. This piece has been produced twice, one version grouted gray (opposite) and one white (below) in order to demonstrate what a striking difference grout color can make to a design. No matter how small the project, grout color is an important consideration. To increase the realism of the effect, some areas of the butterflies' wings were tinted with a darker grout in the white-grouted version.

The way the tiles are laid around an image is almost infinitely variable, but there are some traditional ways to go about it. The method used here—following the lines of the butterflies in a single row, and continuing to follow the shape until the lines of coursing collide—is known as *opus vermiculatum*. *Vermiculatum* has its roots in the Latin word for worm, and refers to the squiggly worm-like shapes the lines of coursing often make.

A small mosaic like this one can be used as a pot stand if you glue felt to the back. Alternatively, you can fix it to a wall with tiling adhesive.

YOU WILL NEED:

- Template from p. 160
- Board, 6 x 6 inches (15 x 15 cm)
- Tracing paper
- Soft pencil (2B or softer)
- Colored pencil
- Tile nippers
- Non-washable P.V.A. glue and brush to apply it
- Rubber gloves
- Gray or white grout, depending on your preference
- Sponge
- Lint-free cloth

MATERIALS

- Vitreous glass tiles, including gemme

indoor projects

Gradual tonal changes look far less jarring than leaps in tone that can also lead to problems in interpreting the image. Here, the shades of yellow in the butterflies' wings gradually become browner at the edges.

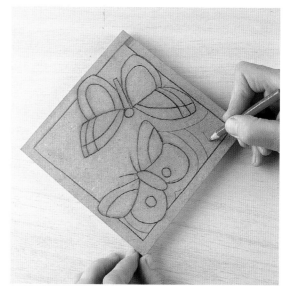

1 **Enlarge the template** on a photocopier, and use a soft pencil to trace the pattern onto the board. (See Drawing and Tracing, p. 20.) Alternatively, you may wish to draw up this simple design freehand. The butterfly is made up of two broadly symmetrical shapes slightly off-set against one another, and crossing a quarter-tile border that runs around the outside of the board.

2 **Having transferred the image** to the board, use a colored pencil to plan the line of the background tiles. In this design, the tiles follow the shape of the butterflies' wings, but you could lay them in a random pattern, in straight lines, or following the outside border tiles inward. The choice is yours.

3 **Assemble the mosaic tiles** and start cutting. The basic tile module for this design is the quarter tile. The easiest way to cut this is to place the nippers on the edge of the tile and squeeze gently. The tile will crack, following the angle at which the nippers are placed.

4 **Fix the tiles** to the board by applying glue to the board, not the tile. Make sure your brush is fine enough to get into those small spaces between the butterfly and the border. Remember: the tiles have to be well stuck down. The grout is a matrix between the tiles, it does not act as an adhesive itself.

6 **When the mosaic is dry**, buff it up with a dry lint-free cloth.

5 **Mix the grout** to a stiffish consistency and apply it to the finished piece, filling all the holes. When you have a small piece like this, you can grout with your hands rather than with a grouting squeegee, but always wear rubber gloves to protect your skin. When the piece is fully grouted, clean with a damp sponge and leave to dry.

Memory Tile

This project demonstrates how to incorporate assorted mosaic material and broken pottery—such as these favorite ceramic cups and saucers from the 1970s and the 1950s—into a successful mosaic design. Mosaics made from recycled objects such as broken ceramic tiles and odds and ends of pottery can look like a random jumble. The way to avoid this problem is to make use of the color and texture of the raw material in your design.

Because this Memory Tile is a very personal piece (yours will inevitably look completely different), it is impossible to give clear instructions on how to recreate it. Instead, this project aims to demonstrate by example and give you guidance on how to examine your own valued souvenirs, analyze their qualities, and structure a design around them.

There is no need to grout a panel like this one, but grout does give a sense of completion to a design. Your finished Memory Tile can be displayed indoors or out.

YOU WILL NEED:

- Tile, 12 x 12 inches (30 x 30 cm)
- Soft pencil (2B or softer)
- Colored crayon
- Long-handled tile nippers
- Side tile nippers
- Cement-based adhesive
- Plasterer's small tool
- Grout
- Sponge
- Rubber gloves
- Lint-free cloth

MATERIALS

- Assorted materials such as broken pottery and glazed and unglazed ceramic tiles

Ceramic and glass mosaic of a similar tone helps connect the background and the cups in this Memory Tile. The glaze on the 1950s cup on the left is creamy, making it less intense and less liable to jump out at you than the 1970s cup on the right.

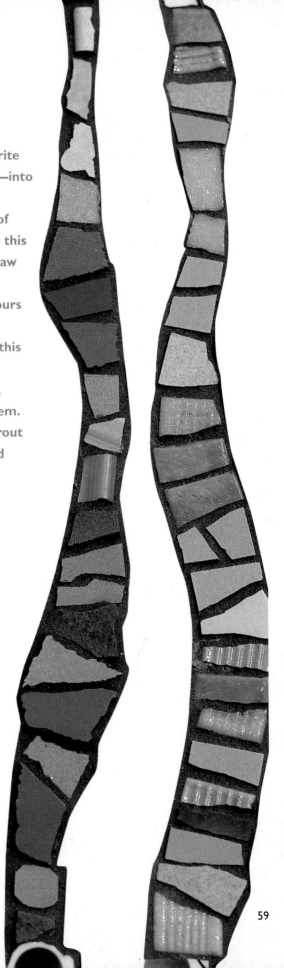

indoor projects

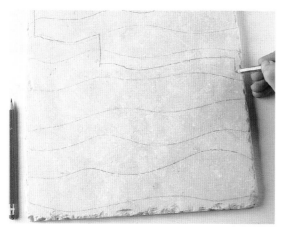

1 **With a pencil,** draw the lines of coursing on your tile. (If you are working on a glazed ceramic tile, turn it over and work on the unglazed back, remembering that cement-based adhesive irons out any slight inconsistencies on the surface.) Next, draw up your design. Use a second color crayon to help you distinguish important design features from the way the background is laid.

2 **When making your design,** think about the color and pattern of the key objects you plan to use, and decide whether you want the design to be based on contrast or fusion between object and background. Choose additional materials accordingly. The challenge of making a Memory Tile is to fuse brightly patterned elements (here the white, black, and brown cup and saucer) with the background.

3 **Your design may** use material with a variety of depths. Here, the cups and saucers are very thin, while the broken dado tile and floor tile are thick. Some difference in level can be disguised by building up thinner items with adhesive, but some tiles may need to be given less depth by cutting off the back with long-handled tile nippers.

4 **Spread a layer** of cement-based adhesive onto the tile with the plasterer's small tool. Raise the shallower materials by applying more adhesive to their backs.

5 **You can experiment** with processes in the Direct Method that are impossible when using the Indirect Method. One of these processes is laying cut tiles on their edge. Cut some of your ceramic tiles into slim lengths and lay them with the rough, cut side up. This adds interesting texture to the panel. It is also a way to create a crisp line.

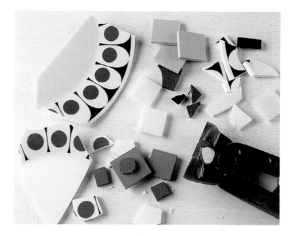

6 **In this design,** the black triangular shapes were separated from the olive-brown dots. This helped create a connection between the triangles on the 1950s cup with the bolder shapes of the 1970s cup.

7 **To make a design based on fusion,** you need to connect your different materials. Here, the connection between the brighter and the more muted cup was made by cutting similar shapes from ceramic and glass mosaic tiles in similar colors.

8 **Build up a patterned line** with your selection of broken pottery and tiles. Here, a white, black, and brown line made from one of the 1970s cups is met by a line of "fake cup." This illusion is created from ceramic and glass tiles in similar shapes and colors.

9 **Think about texture** when designing your mosaic. Here, a piece of marble has been chosen for the slightly crystalline property of its soft riven body, the color and tone of which is similar to that of the large striped glass tile next to the tile nippers. When complete, grout carefully with a gloved hand, then leave to dry. Buff up the completed mosaic with a dry lint-free cloth.

Dragonfly Panel

This decorative panel combines traditional vitreous mosaic tiles and semi-transparent stained glass, whose streaky quality suggests the delicate shimmer of dragonflies' wings as they hover over water. Instead of a violent contrast of color between insect and background, this panel takes a subtle approach. The background is laid in tones that pick up those in the stained glass so that the difference between insect and background is more a matter of scale than of color. The joints between wing sections are intended to suggest their fragmented skeletal form. The mosaic is set onto a mirror so as to retain as much transparency as possible, without actually being see-through.

A final consideration here relates to the striation of the glass. Stained glass like this is not the same on both sides. It is designed with one side, rather than both sides, as the intended viewpoint. This means that you cannot—having completed the wings on one side of the dragonfly—simply turn the glass over to produce a symmetrical image for the other. You have to find sections that appear to streak in the opposite direction within a single sheet of glass. This is something to bear in mind when choosing and buying the stained glass, or your dragonfly may look strangely asymmetrical.

PROJECT TOP TIPS

Laying transparent vitreous glass tiles onto a mirror can produce exciting results. For example, in the body of the dragonfly, ordinary yellow mosaic tiles take on an almost golden luster.

YOU WILL NEED:

- Pencil
- Tracing paper
- Template from p. 160
- Fine non-permanent marker
- Glass cutter
- Tile cutter
- Tile nippers
- Mirror as base 10$\frac{1}{2}$ x 10$\frac{1}{2}$ inches (26.5 x 26.5 cm)
- Clear silicone
- Rubber gloves
- Gray grout
- Sponge
- Lint-free cloth

MATERIALS

- Sheets of stained glass, transparent glass, and opaque glass; vitreous glass tiles, including transparent yellow tiles

1 **With a pencil,** trace the dragonfly onto a sheet of paper. Although the mosaic will be fixed directly onto a mirror, it is best to plan the design on paper rather than on the mirrored surface, whose reflective properties can make a lack of symmetry less evident. Cut the glass down to shapes roughly the size of the wings. (Any errors of judgment must be in making the wings larger, rather than smaller!) Treat the striated glass symmetrically. The wings will look odd if they have stripes along their length on one side and along their width on the other.

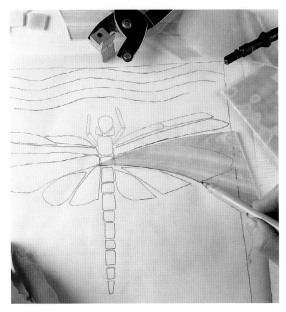

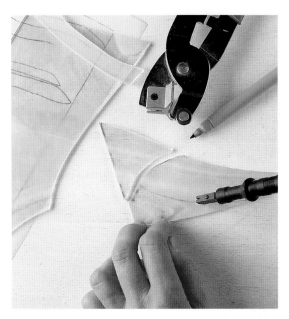

2 Use the drawn dragonfly as a model for how to cut the wings. Using a fine, non-permanent marker, lay a piece of roughly shaped stained glass over the drawing and sketch out the wing's shape.

3 Press firmly along this line with the glass cutter.

4 Place the glass between the jaws of a score-and-snap tile cutter, and break it along the scored line. You need to be precise because these cuts are not heavily disguised by the grout. Practice with some off-cuts before embarking on the real thing.

5 Lay the glass pieces over the template, building up the design section by section. If necessary, use tile nippers to even out the edges of the glass.

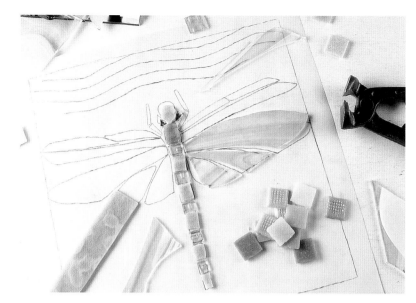

6 **The body of the dragonfly** is made partly from transparent yellow vitreous glass (whose color is purer when laid onto a mirror) and partly from stained glass. To create the mosaic-sized pieces for the slender body, cut a narrow strip of stained glass with the tile cutter, then divide it into tiles using tile nippers. Nip the transparent yellow tiles into quarters.

7 **When you are happy with the design,** transfer it to the mirror. Start by laying out the dragonfly's body in the center, as this is the point of focus. (You may find it helpful to measure the distance from the edges of the mirror tile to position it accurately.) Apply a layer of silicone to the stained glass. Silicone can mute the transparency of the glass, and the wings will adhere well with very little silicone, but you then risk the problem of grout seeping beneath the glass. Either apply silicone all the way around the wings to avoid this potential problem, or make your grout firm so that it is less likely to seep under the tiles.

8 **Start work on the background.**
This is laid in gently curving lines that echo the ripples of water. Divide the tiles into quarters and stick them to the mirror. Note that on everything apart from the dragonfly wings you should put silicone onto the mirror, not the tile. The tile colors are similar in tone and color to the dragonfly, so the wings seem almost camouflaged. This makes the luster of the wings even more exciting when they catch the light. When the design is complete, leave to dry for about 24 hours.

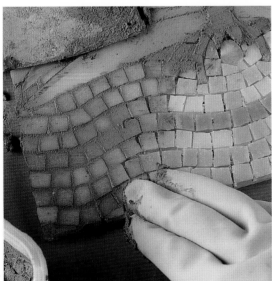

9 **Once entirely dry** (silicone retains a slight flexibility to the touch, unlike cement-based adhesive), grout the mosaic. For the reasons given in Step 7, make the grout a firm consistency. Wearing rubber gloves, grout the mosaic by hand.

10 **Sponge off excess grout** with a well squeezed-out sponge. If the sponge is too wet, you may undo the benefits of using a firm grout, with potentially disastrous consequences. When dry, buff up with a dry lint-free cloth.

Pumpkin Table

This mosaic design is one of the more complex in this book, so try one or two simpler ones before embarking upon it. It is a design that demonstrates something about tone (making bright and dark colors readable against a dark background), cutting (smaller for fine details, larger for emphasis), and color interest (choose a range of tones in one area of the palette to overcome the monotony of flat color, and replicate the shimmery effects of natural materials). Once you have decided on a series of colors around which to structure a design, it can add an element of interest to introduce a "rogue color." This is the job the white flowers do here. It is unlikely that you would ever see flowers and fruit on a single plant, but the flowers bring a note of liveliness to the design that it would lack without them. Don't worry too much about being realistic!

You don't have to cut each tile precisely the way it was cut here—that would make your task infinitely harder—but use the photographs as a guide to color and structure. Don't cut your tiles too small: the centers of the leaves and the little tendrils are the only places where really fine cutting is required.

YOU WILL NEED:

- Masking tape
- Tabletop, 16 x 16 inches (40 x 40 cm)
- Paintbrush
- Black emulsion paint
- Soft pencil (2B or softer)
- Tracing paper
- Template from p. 161
- Tile nippers
- Non-washable P.V.A. glue and brush to apply it
- Rubber gloves
- Gray grout
- Grouting squeegee
- Sponge
- Lint-free cloth

MATERIALS

- Vitreous glass tiles

> **PROJECT TOP TIPS**
>
> In mosaic designs, you should always begin with the main feature. The main image should never be compromised by the background. This is particularly important in an intricate design, such as the Pumpkin Table shown here.

1 **Mask the perimeter** of the board—a layer of paint can interfere with adhesion—then paint the frame, the back of the board, and the table legs. When the paint has dried, remove the masking tape.

2 **With a soft pencil** and tracing paper, transfer the Pumpkin design onto the board. (See Drawing and Tracing, p. 20.)

3 **Create the leaves** by nipping the tiles into quarters. Apply lines of P.V.A. glue to the board, not the tiles. Fix the pale outer lines of each leaf, then the central vein, making sure you leave a consistent gap between them for the main leaf color. Note that the light tone of the leaf edge occasionally changes to an even lighter tone, adding to the delicacy of the leaves.

4 **The basic unit** of this design is the quarter-cut mosaic tile, but to make the delicate outer lines and inner veins of the leaves you will occasionally need to cut finer than this. To do this, cut a tile in half, then in half again (creating a quarter tile), then cut the finer flaring shapes from these. The order in which you should work is: leaves (inner, then outer, then in-between), tendrils, flowers, pumpkins, then background.

5 **Add yellow highlights** to the pumpkin (just a small accent of color can help create a sense of form) and use varying whites in the flowers. It is interesting to see the vibrancy of the ungrouted design. For all its ability to unify a design and its practical properties, grout does mute the color of mosaic.

6 **Put on rubber gloves** before applying the grout with a grouting squeegee, pushing the grout into the joints between the tiles. Scrape any surplus grout from the surface of the piece with the squeegee and put it back into the container.

7 **Sponge the excess** grout from the surface of the mosaic. Wet the sponge, then squeeze as dry as possible. Clean in a series of single sweeps, and at the end of each sweep turn the sponge. When all sides of the sponge have been used, clean it in a bucket of water and re-squeeze dry. Continue until the surface is completely clean, then leave the mosaic to dry. When the grout is dry (usually after a couple of hours), buff up the mosaic with a dry lint-free cloth.

Smalti Dish

This colorful project demonstrates how to
cover a shallow dish in smalti, an enameled
glass that was used on the great Byzantine wall
mosaics. Smalti has an extraordinary intensity
of color and is very effective in simple
patterns, as shown here. Because it is a
material that has an uneven surface, it is best
fixed into a bed of cement-based adhesive.
Choose a dish with a simple shape, as
complicated curves are difficult to cover.

YOU WILL NEED:

- Terra-cotta dish, 10 inches
  (25.5 cm) in diameter
- Soft pencil (2B or softer)
- Cement-based adhesive
- Palette knife
- Tile nippers
- Paint
- Paintbrush

MATERIALS

- Smalti

indoor projects

1 **Sketch out a pattern** on the terra-cotta dish with the pencil, and select the colors you intend to use.

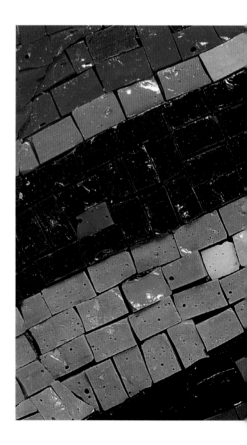

2 **Apply a bed** of prepared adhesive to a small area of the inside base of the dish. (If you cover too large an area, the adhesive will start to skin over and won't be usable.) The adhesive should be about ¹⁄₈th inch (3 mm) thick to allow for the unevenness of the surface of the smalti. Cut the smalti to size by placing the nippers across the whole width of the tile rather than just the edge as you would with vitreous glass tiles. Firmly press the smalti into the adhesive bed.

3 **When you have covered** the base of the dish, carefully apply adhesive in small sections to the sides and rim. It is easiest to do the sides and rim at the same time to ensure a neat junction. Make sure there is plenty of adhesive under the smalti at the rim, since this will be vulnerable to knocks. Leave the dish to dry for at least two hours.

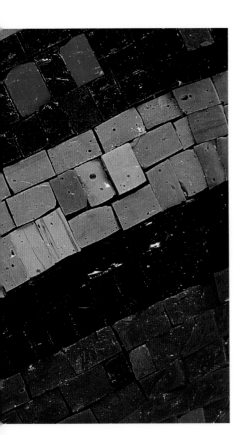

4 **When the adhesive is dry,** paint the outside of the dish a matching color.

Candleholders

These little candleholders are made from plain, straight-sided beakers. It is a good idea to use simple shapes like these so as to avoid complicated cutting. This project uses strips of stained glass and translucent mosaic pieces that allow the flickering light of the candle to shine through. Small pieces of gold mosaic are used to give a reflective quality to the piece. The black grout that fills in the gaps gives the finished object a stained-glass quality, but you could use white grout for a fresher effect or even leave the piece ungrouted. The vertical emphasis of the design allows the strips of stained glass to follow the curve of the beaker.

YOU WILL NEED:

- Small glass beaker
- Brown paper
- Pencil
- Scissors
- Glass cutter
- Ruler
- Tile cutter
- Double-wheeled tile nippers
- Latex gloves
- Clear silicone glue
- Spreading tool
- Small screwdriver
- Black grout
- Sponge
- Rubber gloves

MATERIALS

- Stained glass; translucent mosaic tiles

1 Make a paper template by wrapping a piece of brown paper around the glass beaker and marking the line of the top of the beaker with a pencil. Cut the paper along this line.

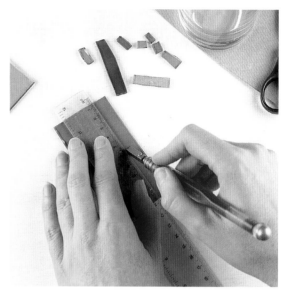

2 Cut the stained glass into narrow strips. First score the surface of the glass using a glass cutter and a ruler, then snap off the strip with a tile cutter. Avoid making wide strips since these won't lie flat against the surface of the beaker and will look awkward.

3 Cut some of the mosaic tiles in half with double-wheeled tile nippers. (Double-wheeled tile nippers are more accurate and can be used to cut thinner strips than ordinary side tile nippers.)

4 Lay out the glass strips and tiles on the brown paper template, cutting them to fit with the double-wheeled tile nippers.

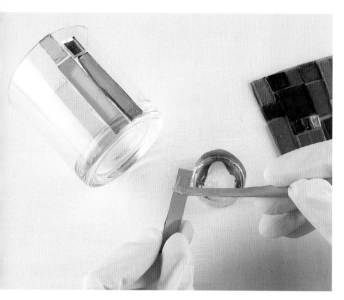

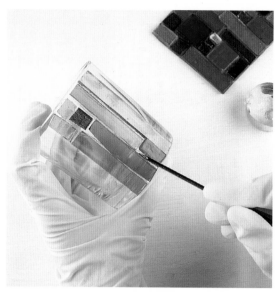

5 **Transfer the glass pieces** from the paper template to the beaker. Put on some latex gloves, then spread a small amount of clear silicone glue over the back of the glass pieces with a spreading tool. Be sure to cover the whole surface or air bubbles will be trapped behind the glass. Place each strip on the glass beaker and press gently, forcing out any air bubbles you can see.

6 **If the silicone comes up** between the joints, carefully scrape it out with a small screwdriver or other pointed tool.

7 **When you have stuck down** all the pieces, set aside the beaker until the glue is completely dry. This usually takes a couple of hours, but will vary according to the ambient temperature. When completely dry, grout the piece using your hands protected in rubber gloves.

8 **Remove the excess grout** with a damp sponge and give the piece a final polish with a dry lint-free cloth.

Mirrored Sconce

This project exploits the various reflective qualities of glass and mirror by combining textured glass with colored glass and translucent glass mosaic. The glittering potential of these materials is enhanced by fixing them to a mirror backing that allows light to shine through them as well as onto their surfaces. Small, circular mirrors are set into the strips of textured glass to provide spots of pure reflection against the more refracted overall surface. Flickering candlelight adds a subtle movement that animates the final effect.

The piece is left ungrouted so that the sides of the glass pieces can add sparkle and create a sense of depth. Copper strip protects the exposed edges and provides a frame that is sympathetic both in color and reflectivity. If you can't get hold of copper strip, metallic adhesive tape makes a good alternative.

YOU WILL NEED:

- 2 pieces M.D.F.
  base: 6 x 6 x ¹/₂ inches
  (150 x 150 x 12 mm)
  back: 14 x 6 x ¹/₂ inches
  (350 x 150 x 12 mm)
- Wood glue
- 1 inch (2.5 cm) nails
- Hammer
- 2 sheets mirror
  base: 6 x 6 inches
  (15 x 15 cm)
  back: 13¹/₄ x 6 inches
  (34 x 15 cm)
- Latex gloves
- Clear silicone glue
- Double-wheeled tile nippers
- Glass cutter
- Ruler
- Tile cutter
- Spreading tool
- Small screwdriver
- Copper edging strip
  (optional) 4 feet 3 inches
  (1.3 m)
- Copper hardboard pins

MATERIALS

- Vitreous glass tiles;
  sheets of clear textured
  glass and stained glass;
  round mirror tiles

indoor projects

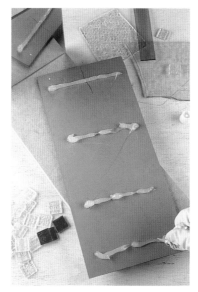

1 **Make an L-shaped base** by gluing and nailing together the two pieces of M.D.F. Drill a hole in the back board so that the piece can be hung over a nail in the wall.

2 **Cut or buy two pieces** of mirror glass to fit both the back and base of the sconce. Wearing latex gloves, apply lines of silicone glue about 3 inches (7.5 cm) apart to the back of the mirrors.

3 **Place the first piece** of mirror on the base of the sconce and press into position so it is firmly stuck in place. Repeat with the back piece.

4 **To cut the clear and colored glass** into narrow strips, first score it with a glass cutter along the straight edge of a ruler.

5 **Snap the glass** along the scored line using the snappers on an ordinary score-and-snap tile cutter. Prepare the other mosaic pieces by cutting the vitreous glass tiles in half with tile nippers.

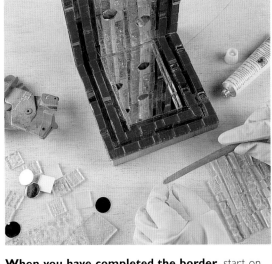

6 **Protect your hands** with the gloves again, then apply a thin coat of clear silicone glue to the back of the glass pieces with the spreading tool. Be sure to cover the whole of the surface or air bubbles will be trapped behind the glass. Press the pieces down onto the surface of the mirror, forcing out any air bubbles you can see. Create a row of red glass tiles, adding the occasional small brown and gold glass piece. Next, make up a row of different shades of clear green glass. Repeat these two rows.

7 **When you have completed the border,** start on the clear central area. Lay out the strips of glass on your work surface before sticking so that you can be sure they will fit into the space available. First fix the circular mirrors with the silicone glue.

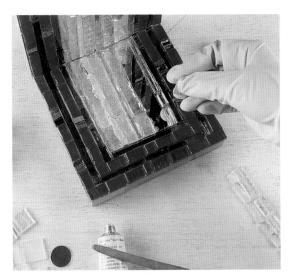

8 **Cut the strips of glass** to fit around the round mirror tiles. Apply silicone glue to the back of the strips of glass, then press them into position on the surface of the mirror. When complete, set aside the sconce until the glue is completely dry. This usually takes a couple of hours, but will vary according to the ambient temperature.

9 **To frame the piece,** measure the length of copper strip you need to go around the edge of the back panel and cut off the right amount. Starting at one end, hammer copper hardboard pins through the copper strip into the M.D.F. board. Make sure the nails are not too close to the edge of the board or they will not hold and may damage the mirror backing. Continue nailing at about 2 inch (5 cm) intervals, making sure the strip is fixed as tightly to the edge of the mosaic as possible. Repeat around the edge of the base of the sconce.

Kitchen Clock

This design shows how you can create the illusion of a three-dimensional shape in mosaic. The pieces of fruit appear to sit on the plate, making you feel you could pick them up and eat them. The addition of the clock hands, however, belies the illusion and draws attention to the actual flatness of the surface.

One of the techniques used to create the impression of form is shading. On the pear, this is achieved by choosing a blend of green tiles that shade smoothly from dark to light. These tiles are then laid along a slightly curving line across the fruit to suggest its rounded shape. The transition from dark to light is staggered on alternate rows in order to soften the effect and avoid vertical lines that would fight against the emphasis of the curving lines.

On the fig, the lines of laying (see p. 16) follow the outline of the fruit, with a dark line on one side and a light line on the other to emphasize the form. The shape is filled in with lines of alternating tones to suggest the fig's slightly ridged surface. Blue and tones of purple are used to represent the bloom on the skin. The other illusionistic trick is the use of shadows on the surface of the plate that separate the objects from their background. This is simply done by changing the tone of the tiles used while maintaining the pattern.

YOU WILL NEED:

- Drawing paper
- Colored pencils
- Template from p. 162
- Tracing paper
- Soft pencil (2B or softer)
- Brown paper
- Scissors
- Protractor
- Tile nippers
- Washable P.V.A. glue diluted 50:50 with water and brush to apply it
- Gray grout
- Rubber gloves
- Sponge
- 16 inch (40 cm) diameter framed board with a hole drilled in the center
- Cement-based adhesive
- Small notched spreader
- Small screwdriver
- Lint-free cloth
- Clock mechanism and hands

MATERIALS

- Vitreous glass tiles

1 **To make your own design,** or amend this or any of the designs given in the book, make a color sketch to help you choose which colored tiles to use and assess the quantities you will need. Remember that when using the Indirect Method (as here), you must reverse the design when transferring it to the brown paper. This is because you make the mosaic back-to-front before fixing it onto the board.

2 **Enlarge the template** on a photocopier, and use a soft pencil to trace the pattern onto the rough side of a circle of brown paper cut to fit the board.

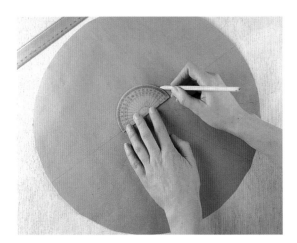

3 **If you want to create** your own design, set out the spacings for the clock divisions using a protractor. Mark off 30 degree intervals and draw lines radiating out from the center point. You can place the minute marks any distance in from the edge of the circle so long as they are consistently placed.

4 **Lay the outer band first,** since this defines the extent of the inside panel. Cut the tiles into quarters with the tile nippers, then stick them face down onto the brown paper. Apply the P.V.A. glue to the paper, not the tiles. To make the round minute markers, nibble off the corners of whole tiles with the tile nippers and keep nibbling until you have formed a smooth curve. (You might find it easiest to use the back of the tile nippers for this.)

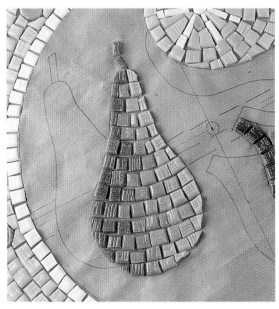

5 **Lay the fruit.** When making the pear, try to stagger the vertical joints by using half tiles where necessary. These lines will be less conspicuous than ones accidentally created when the joints line up.

6 **When you have completed the fruit,** lay the background. Start from one of the ruled lines that runs across the center so that the clock hands can emerge from a hole that you create between two rows. When you come to a shadow line as shown here, cut the tile to follow the line but continue in a darker tone.

7 **When all the tiles** are attached and the glue is dry, you are ready to fix the piece. Spread grout across the back of the mosaic with your hands protected in rubber gloves.

8 **Remove the excess grout** with a damp sponge. Clean in a series of single sweeps, and at the end of each sweep turn the sponge. When all sides of the sponge have been used, clean and re-squeeze dry. Continue until grout is left only in the joints.

9 **Spread cement-based adhesive** over the board (avoiding the central hole) using a small notched spreader. Spread the adhesive to the edges and comb it afterward to achieve an even thickness of bed.

10 **Turn over the pre-grouted mosaic** into the adhesive and press down firmly to expel pockets of air that can prevent proper bonding.

11 **Wet the backing paper** and leave for approximately ten minutes so the glue can dissolve. Carefully peel the paper back, starting at one edge and pulling the paper parallel to the mosaic surface, not up and away from the adhesive bed. Lay your other hand on the mosaic to push down any pieces that may become dislodged. When all the paper has been removed, wash the mosaic with a damp sponge to remove surface grout.

12 **When the piece is dry,** re-grout it to fill in any gaps.

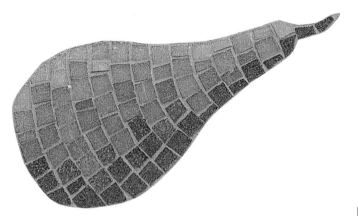

13 **Clean off excess grout** with a damp sponge, always using a clean face so that the grout is not spread back over the surface. Clean out the hole in the center with a small screwdriver, making sure there is no sandy residue left to clog up the clock mechanism.

14 **When the piece is dry,** buff up with a lint-free cloth. Attach the clock mechanism to the back of the board and fit the hands over the protruding spindle.

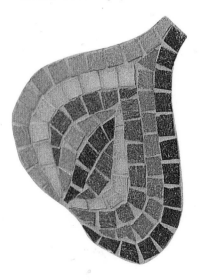

Ceramic Sampler

This panel is made from off-cuts of ceramic tiles as well as whole tiles, and demonstrates that how you cut tiles is less important than how you lay them. The peculiar shapes of the ceramic oddments are given a rhythm by keeping an.even gap between them. The design is intended to be a series of experiments with different laying techniques, like a sampler in needlework.

Even though this is an exercise in using randomly cut material, you should still keep an eye on the balance of colors in the sampler. Notice how the white tiles in the top left-hand corner of this sampler dominate the design, thanks to their larger scale and machine-made shape. The white, and its adjoining panel in brown stripes, balance the brighter browns and yellows in the bottom row.

indoor projects

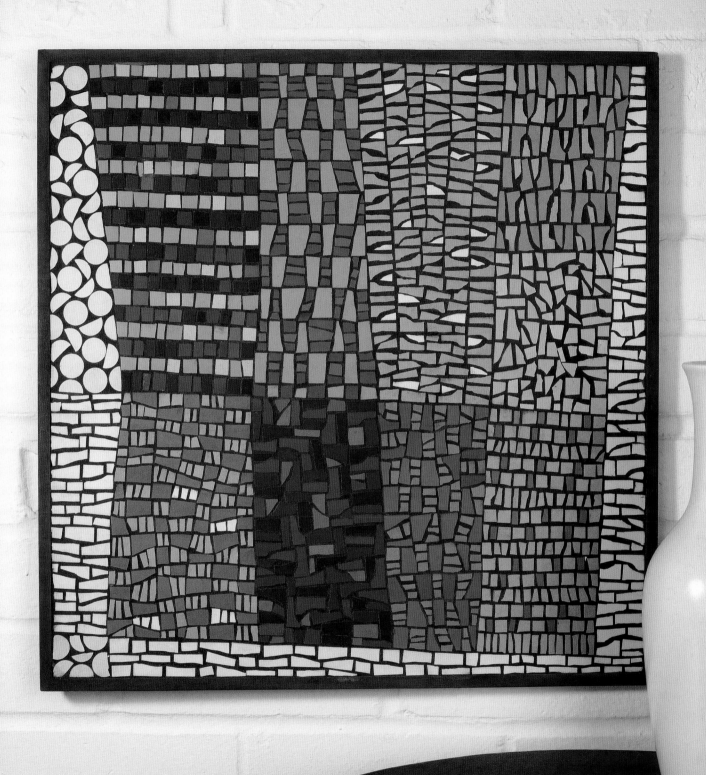

1 **Cut a sheet of brown paper** to fit the board. Sketch your design on the rough (not shiny) side of the paper with the permanent marker: do not use a washable pen because it might stain the tiles. Cut the tiles with the tile nippers and fix them in position, face down. Remember to apply the P.V.A. glue to the paper, not the tiles.

2 **When you have completed the design,** put on rubber gloves and pre-grout the mosaic. Push grout into the joints, leaving as little on the back of the tiles as possible. Wet a sponge, then squeeze it until nearly dry. Sweep the sponge across the mosaic, turning after each sweep to a clean face of the sponge. When all sides of the sponge have been used, clean it in the bucket and repeat until the surface of the mosaic is entirely clean.

3 **Apply adhesive to the board** with the trowel. You are applying the adhesive properly if you hear a scraping sound as you pull the trowel across the board.

4 **Pick up the pre-grouted mosaic** by diagonally opposed corners and lay it face down on the adhesive bed. Adjust as necessary. When the mosaic is in place, tap it all over with a flat-bed squeegee to expel pockets of air that can prevent proper bonding.

5 **Wet the backing paper** with a damp sponge and leave for about ten minutes. If the paper starts to dry out (patches of a lighter color will appear), sponge again. When the paper has absorbed all the moisture, start peeling from one corner. Peel the paper flat back on itself (not upward, which can lift tiles). When you have reached halfway across, place the paper back down where it came from and repeat the operation from the other side. If any tiles come up as you peel, simply replace them. When all the paper has been removed, sponge the surface of the tiles. When the surface is clean, leave to dry until the adhesive has cured.

6 **Re-grout the mosaic** as before or with a gloved hand. Be careful, because the mosaic will be fragile.

7 **Sponge off the grout,** remembering to turn and clean the sponge as you did in Step 2. When you are sure the surface is clean, leave it to dry, then buff up the surface of the mosaic with a dry lint-free cloth.

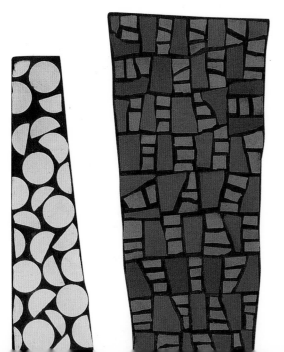

Cityscape

Smalti is one of the most beautiful of all mosaic materials. The glass pieces are made now as they were in Roman times: cut from circular plates that are formed by pouring the molten colored glass onto a flat surface and allowing the plates to cool gradually through a series of different ovens. The resulting material has an intensity of opaque color unmatched by any other, which is why the great mosaics of the Byzantine age—such as St. Mark's in Venice and the churches of Ravenna in Italy—read so clearly and dramatically across large architectural spaces.

Smalti can be difficult to use effectively on a smaller scale because the brightness of the colors can be overpowering in a domestic setting. In this design, small amounts of intense yellow and pink are used in combination with more muted grays and browns so that the bright colors outshine the subtler colors surrounding them but do not fight each other.

The scene is an imaginary cityscape of modern and traditional buildings that uses the rectilinear shapes of the material to form the equally rectangular shapes of the design. The contemporary references in the image contrast with the ancient and traditional associations of the smalti, and the limited use of gold adds richness and sparkle.

YOU WILL NEED:

- Colored pencils
- Drawing paper
- Charcoal stick
- Brown paper
- Template from p. 163
- Scissors
- Washable P.V.A. glue diluted 50:50 with water and brush to apply it
- Double-wheeled tile nippers
- Cement-based adhesive
- Plasterer's small tool
- Board, 16 x 16 inches (40 x 40 cm)
- Rubber gloves
- Sponge
- Small screwdriver

MATERIALS

- Approximately 6¹/₂ pounds (3 kg) smalti; gold vitreous glass tiles

1 **Make sketches** with colored pencils on drawing paper. Refer to the available smalti colors and match them to your pencil colors. Quick sketches will help you work out a balanced design, particularly where you intend to use lots of different colors.

2 **With the charcoal stick,** transfer your design onto the rough side of a piece of brown paper cut to the size of the board. (Alternatively, use the template on p. 163.) Reverse the design if you want it to be the same way around as your sketch. The charcoal drawing will be a rough guide, since the exact sizes and positions of the buildings will be dictated by the sizes of the smalti. Because you're using the Indirect Method, you can make amendments as you work and before the mosaic is finally fixed.

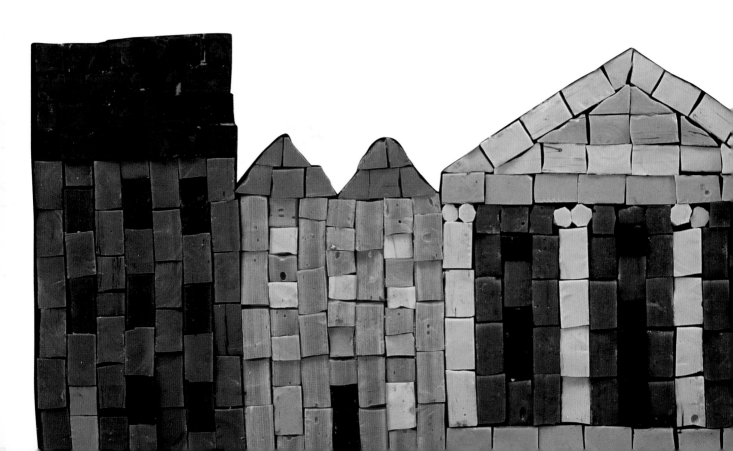

3 **Start by laying out** the bottom row so that most of the buildings are made from whole tiles, and cut tiles only where unavoidable. This mosaic will not be grouted, so the smalti must be laid quite close to each other. Fix them in place with a layer of P.V.A. glue applied to the paper with a small brush.

4 **Continue to work up** the design, using your original colored sketches for guidance.

5 **Use double-wheeled tile nippers** to shape and cut smalti, and remember to stick gold pieces face down at this stage (with their greenish backs showing).

6 **When you come to the sky,** lay the rows from the top of the paper down so that the cut tiles are around the buildings rather than at the edge of the mosaic. Changes can easily be made at this stage by lifting off smalti with a small screwdriver and replacing them with other colors to achieve a better overall balance.

7 **When the mosaic is finished** and the glue dried, fix it to the backing board. Wearing rubber gloves, spread a layer of cement-based adhesive over the board with a plasterer's small tool. The adhesive should be about 1/8th inch (3 mm) thick to allow for the unevenness of the surface of the smalti.

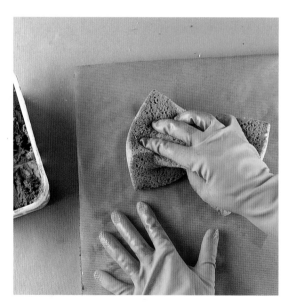

8 **Turn the mosaic over** into the adhesive and wet the backing paper immediately with a damp sponge, pressing down as you do so. The water will soften the paper and allow the smalti to sink into the adhesive bed so that the finished mosaic will have an interesting, uneven surface.

9 **When the water has penetrated** the paper and dissolved the glue, peel back the paper. As you peel, press the individual smalti pieces down to be sure that they are in full contact with the adhesive below. The surface will be sticky, so use a screwdriver to press down the smalti rather than your fingers, which could stick to the mosaic and dislodge the tiles.

10 **Scrape out any adhesive** that comes up between the joints with the screwdriver. This is easiest to do when the adhesive is beginning to dry, which will be after about 30 minutes.

11 **When the adhesive is completely dry** (depending on the brand and temperature this is usually after about four hours), wash off the excess P.V.A. glue from the surface with a wet sponge.

Quilt Table

Many of the designs in this book use a muted palette, but this mosaic has a range of bright colors. With a pattern like this, you need to bear three issues in mind: brightness, tone, and the area of the spectrum from which a color comes. You might be surprised to see how much brighter the orange and blue tiles are than the reds. And although the pink is tonally similar to the turquoise and green, these colors are brighter than the pink. However, the design is really based around browns and blues, and the pink and mauve tiles are the tonal bridge between them.

Another important aspect of the design is the lines along which the mosaic is laid. Each segment (a quarter of a diamond within a square) is laid in an opposing direction. This gives a pleasingly stuttering rhythm to the design. No direction takes precedence; each quarter is in the grip of its neighbor.

If you want to paint the table base and edges, do it before you start work on the mosaic. Remember to mask off the surface first because paint can prevent the adhesive from adhering.

YOU WILL NEED:

- Tabletop, 20 x 20 inches (50 x 50 cm)
- Brown paper
- Ruler
- Pencil
- Permanent marker
- Tile nippers
- Washable P.V.A. glue diluted 50:50 with water and brush to apply it
- Rubber gloves
- Grouting squeegee
- Black grout
- Sponge
- $1/8$ inch (3 mm) notched trowel
- Gray adhesive
- Flat-bed squeegee
- Lint-free cloth

MATERIALS

- Vitreous glass tiles

indoor projects

1 **Draw in a border** about 1 inch (2.5 cm) thick—the design would be less attractive if the points of the diamonds met the edge of the board. Draw up the square grid, then add the diagonal lines. In this design, each square is approximately 3 x 3 inches (8 cm).

2 **Go over the pencil lines** with a permanent marker. Make sure the pen is not water-soluble, or the ink may stain your tiles.

3 **Select your colors** and start to cut the tiles. Since this design is based on a quarter tile repeat, you can cut a large quantity of various colors. This will be quicker than cutting to fit every time you lay tiles.

4 **Stick the tiles face down** along the border, applying glue to the paper not the tiles. In most mosaic designs, you begin with the main feature, then complete the border (if you have one), leaving the background until last. In this design the border gives you a structure within which to work.

5 **Each large square on the table** is divided into four two-color quarters. The sections above and next to the quarter on which you are working are laid in the opposing direction. It is easy to get confused about this, so sketch directional arrows on the paper.

6 **When you have laid** the whole of one eighth (in this case, pale green), lay the interlocking other side (pale purple). Notice how each quarter ends with a whole line of the two colors.

7 **Continue to build up the design,** making sure you have an even spread of color, tone, and intensity. Do not bunch all the dark colors in one corner or place lots of bright colors next to each other. Aim to achieve an overall balance, without repeating particular colors in particular areas.

8 **When the glue has dried,** pre-grout the mosaic. Put on rubber gloves, then mix black grout to a stiffish consistency and apply to the mosaic with a grouting squeegee. Bright colors often retain their vibrancy best when grouted a dark color, as here.

9 **When you have filled all the joints** on the back of the mosaic, remove as much grout as you can with the squeegee. Wet a sponge then squeeze it until it is as dry as possible. Sweep the sponge flat against the mosaic, as this picks up the maximum quantity of grout. Turn after each sweep to a clean face of the sponge. When all sides of the sponge have been used, clean it in the bucket and repeat until the mosaic is completely clean.

10 **Apply adhesive to the board** with the notched trowel. (Press the trowel firmly to the board to prevent too much adhesive from being applied.)

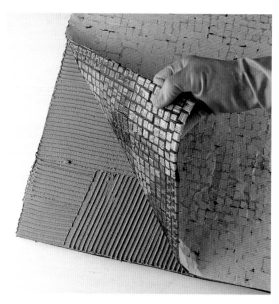

11 **Pick up the pre-grouted mosaic** by two diagonally opposing corners, turn it over, and lay it into the bed of adhesive. (You can easily orient the remaining two corners this way.)

12 **Tap the mosaic** all over with a flat-bed squeegee to expel pockets of air that can prevent proper bonding.

13 **Wet the backing paper** with a damp sponge and leave for about ten minutes. If the paper starts to dry out (if patches of a lighter color appear), sponge again.

14 **Once the paper is thoroughly soaked,** peel the paper flat back on itself. When you have reached halfway, place the paper back where it came from and repeat the operation from the other side. This prevents unpredictable stresses on the tiles, which can cause them to lift. Sponge off the grout in order to achieve an even grout surface. (Patchy grout can be difficult to remove it if it is allowed to dry on the tiles.) When you are sure the surface is clean, leave to dry until the adhesive has cured. Once the mosaic has dried (generally after about 24 hours), re-grout, sponge off, and leave to dry. When dry, buff up with a dry lint-free cloth.

Patio Table

The muted colors of this elegant table make it usable in the home or outside on a patio or balcony. Restrained colors, such as the ones used here, often work best outdoors. They look natural and don't compete with the constantly varying color combinations that seasonal changes bring. However, if you plan to leave this table outdoors for extended periods, you must ensure that the board is made of a material that can withstand such conditions, and that the adhesive you use is compatible with your board. (See pp. 28 and 30 for more details.)

The circular tabletop was the starting point for this design. Sometimes round ceramic tiles were used whole, sometimes they were cut up, but the circular shape links them all. The design's asymmetry is part of its appeal. There is something pleasing about irregularity in a mosaic as long as the space between the tiles is even and the tiles are carefully shaped. This effect is easier to achieve with ceramic tiles, which are slightly easier to cut than those made from vitreous glass.

YOU WILL NEED:

- 20 inch (50 cm) diameter framed tabletop
- Masking tape
- Paint
- Paintbrush
- Template from p. 164
- Scissors
- Tracing paper
- Brown paper
- Soft pencil (2B or softer)
- Tile nippers
- Washable P.V.A. glue diluted 50:50 with water and brush to apply it
- Rubber gloves
- Gray grout
- Palette knife
- Grouting squeegee
- Flat-bed squeegee
- Sponge
- $\frac{1}{8}$ inch (3 mm) notched trowel
- Cement-based adhesive
- Lint-free cloth

MATERIALS

- Square and round ceramic tiles; vitreous glass tiles, including gemme

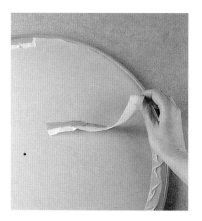

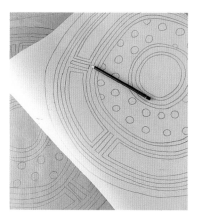

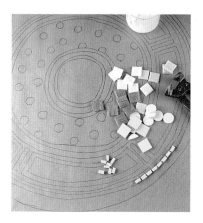

1 **Mask the perimeter** of the board—a layer of paint can interfere with adhesion—then paint the frame, the back of the board, and the table legs. When the paint has dried, remove the masking tape.

2 **Enlarge the template** on a photocopier, and use a soft pencil to trace the pattern onto a sheet of brown paper cut to the same size as your board. Alternatively, you may wish to draw up your own design. (See Drawing and Tracing, p. 20.)

3 **Choose your tiles.** Lay the structural lines of the design first. To make these, cut a ceramic tile in half and in half again, then cut each quarter tile in half to make eighths. Apply a line of glue to the paper and fix the pieces of tile in place.

4 **Laying the structural lines first** can sometimes make the paper buckle, as this photograph illustrates. The glue may be too wet and the paper may be stretching. Or you may be laying the tiles too tightly, causing the paper to expand. If it happens, just boldly lay the tiles over the buckled surface.

PROJECT TOP TIPS

This picture shows alternative ways of shaping tiles to fit the boxes of the outer circle. If you are having problems cutting a tile to fit, lay the tile in the gap and mark it with a pencil, as shown here, before cutting it to fill the space.

5 **Once you have laid the structural lines,** lay the background. Cut up round, ceramic tiles and glue them into the central circle and the broad outer ring. Make round shapes from square ceramic tiles and glue these in the inner ring. (The slight unevenness of these hand-cut shapes makes the design more interesting.) Cut white ceramic tiles into petal shapes (see p. 14). When the design is complete, leave it to dry.

6 **Put on rubber gloves,** then pre-grout the mosaic with a stiffish mix of grout. The grout used here is gray, even though the mosaic is largely pale in tone. The joints between the tiles are like pencil marks on a drawing: they delicately outline the pattern. Having cut the tiles so carefully to achieve this effect, you don't want to lose it by using white grout.

7 **Trowel adhesive evenly over the board.** Pick up the pre-grouted mosaic, turn it over, and lay it into the bed of adhesive. Tap the mosaic all over with a flat-bed squeegee to expel pockets of air that can prevent proper bonding. Wet the backing paper with a damp sponge. Leave it for ten minutes to absorb the water, re-wetting if it dries out. Peel the paper off, first from one side, then the other, flapping it back flat over the mosaic as you change sides. Sponge clean and leave to dry.

8 **Go over the mosaic** with a damp sponge so the dry grout doesn't suck the moisture out of the new batch of grout. Re-grout from the front, filling all the little holes you missed the first time.

9 **Remove as much grout** as possible with the squeegee, then sponge the mosaic clean. Sweep the sponge flat against the tiles, and turn it every time you make a fresh sweep across the surface. When all sides have been used, rinse it in the bucket and repeat until the mosaic is completely clean. (Sponge lightly or you may start to remove grout from between the tiles.) Leave to dry, then buff up with a dry lint-free cloth.

Striped Backsplash

Most of the projects in this book are made with cut tiles, but mosaics made with whole tiles can be equally attractive and have the virtue of being quicker to complete than conventional cut-piece work. However, you must bear in mind the size and shape of whole tiles when you plan this design. When you create a backsplash to be fixed in a particular position, make sure you work to the size of the nearest whole tile. If this leaves an unpleasant gap, consider framing the board and allowing the frame to fill the space. Seeing cut mosaic tiles along one edge of the board can make something pleasing look messy.

Grout can have a strong influence on how colors read together. If you choose the wrong grout, colors that previously looked harmonious can jangle. This is generally due to a contrast of tone. Try to match the grout's tone to that of the tiles. The tiles used in this design are mid-tone, so a mid-gray is the best color to use. You may want to tint a grout (for example, blue to match a design predominantly made with blue tiles) and this can work, but there can be attendant problems. (See p.19 for more about choosing and using grout.)

For this design you need to make a grid on paper, using a sheet of mosaic tiles as your guide to spacing. So don't soak the tiles off the sheet until you have drawn up the grid! This mosaic is made in two sections.

YOU WILL NEED:

- Scissors
- Brown paper
- Exterior-grade board, 40 x 16 inches (1 m x 40 cm)
- Permanent marker
- Pencil
- Ruler
- Washable P.V.A. glue diluted 50:50 with water and brush to apply it
- Stanley knife
- Rubber gloves
- White adhesive
- 1/8 inch (3 mm) notched trowel
- Gray grout
- Grouting squeegee
- Flat-bed squeegee
- Sponge
- Lint-free cloth

MATERIALS

- Vitreous glass tiles

You can make this backsplash by sticking down rows of tesserae sliced from sheets of single-color glass tiles, but this isn't a good idea. A design created from rows of tiles in a single color will not be as interesting as one made with tiles that have slight variations of shade. This is why you should make the backsplash with individual tiles in close tones.

1 **Cut a sheet of brown paper** to fit the board, then mark the back of the paper (the shiny side) with letters A and B and arrows so you will know how the design fits together later. (As a rule, it is unwise to make sections bigger than about a 1 1/2 feet (45 cm) square until you have more experience in handling mosaic.) Make sure the arrows point in the same direction.

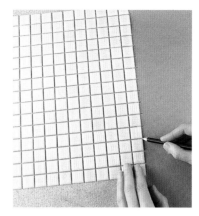

2 **With a pencil,** mark the spacing of the tiles you plan to use on the rough side of the paper. The easiest way to do this is to use a sheet of mosaic as your model. Draw up a grid based on the spacing between the tiles on a sheet. Join up the marks with a ruler. (Now you can soak off the tiles.)

3 **Stick the tiles** onto the grid, making sure they line up evenly in both directions. Be moderate in your application of P.V.A. glue to the paper, or it will stretch. While this is not a disaster, it will make lining up the tiles more difficult.

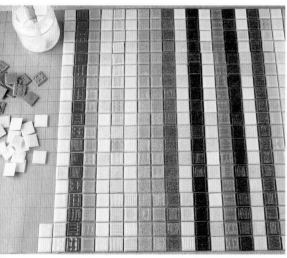

4 **As you work across the design,** laying and sticking the tiles, make sure your choice of colors has an overall balance. (For example, the bright red tiles on the left effectively balance out the darker lines to the right.) Continue laying tiles until the paper is covered, then leave to dry. Use a Stanley knife to cut the mosaic in half, then pre-grout section A.

5 **Apply adhesive** to the area of board to be covered by section A right away. Wearing gloves, mix the adhesive to a stiffish consistency before troweling it onto the board. Use a white adhesive to retain the bright color of the semi-transparent tiles. (A gray adhesive will give the backsplash a more muted appearance.)

Trowel the adhesive onto the board. Press the notched trowel firmly to the board to prevent too much adhesive being applied. An uneven application of adhesive can result in an unevenly tiled surface, which is very noticeable when the design is based on an even grid.

6 **Pick up the pre-grouted section A,** turn it over, and lay it into the bed of adhesive. Tap the mosaic all over with a flat-bed squeegee to expel pockets of air that can prevent proper bonding. Pre-grout section B of the mosaic and fix it to the board in the same way.

7 **Apply both sections** to the board before you sponge off the paper. (On large mosaics with several sections, you should wet the paper, peel, and sort out any potential problems—such as loose tiles, holes, and uneven joints—as you fix each section.) Sponge well, then leave the paper to absorb the water for approximately ten minutes.

8 **Peel off the paper** when it is evenly dark across the entire area. If the paper starts to dry out (patches of a lighter color appear), sponge again. Work from the edge to the center, peeling the paper flat to the board. Halfway across, peel in from the other side until you meet the area you have already peeled. Once the paper has been peeled away, sponge the mosaic with a damp sponge that has been squeezed as dry as possible. When you are sure the surface is clean, leave to dry until the adhesive has cured.

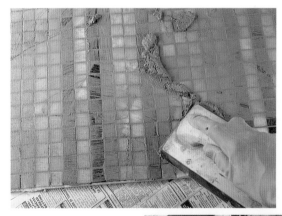

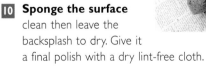

9 **Go over the mosaic** with a damp sponge so the dry grout doesn't suck the moisture out of the new batch of grout. Re-grout from the front, filling all the little holes you missed the first time.

10 **Sponge the surface** clean then leave the backsplash to dry. Give it a final polish with a dry lint-free cloth.

Circles Backsplash

This backsplash demonstrates that something simple can be enlivened by following one or two elementary principles. The design is based on repeated circles: colored rings surrounded by white. The combination could be hard and jarring, but is softened by the variety of white tones used. As the circles radiate outward, the tone of the colored bands darkens. Like the white bands, these tend not to be bands of a single color. These variations of shade help create a "dancing" effect.

The similarity of palette between this and the Striped Backsplash (see p. 110) allows you to compare the effects of a striped and a circular pattern. Choose colors to suit your own taste, bearing in mind that white is always a fresh color to use in a bathroom or kitchen. Like the Striped Backsplash, this mosaic is made in two sections.

YOU WILL NEED:

- Scissors
- Brown paper
- Exterior-grade board, 40 x 16 inches (1 m x 40 cm)
- Pencil
- Ruler
- Pair of compasses
- Tile nippers
- Washable P.V.A. glue diluted 50:50 with water and brush to apply it
- Permanent marker
- Stanley knife
- Rubber gloves
- Gray grout
- Grouting squeegee
- White adhesive
- 1/8 inch (3 mm) notched trowel
- Sponge
- Lint-free cloth

MATERIALS

- Vitreous glass tiles

indoor projects

1 **Cut a sheet of brown paper** to fit the board. Working on the rough side of the paper, divide up the area into a number of sections by halving, then quartering, squares. The idea is to produce a pattern that relates to the size of your own backsplash.

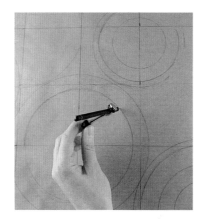

2 **Once the paper is divided up,** place the pair of compasses on an intersection and start to set out your circles. The circles here are not arranged strictly symmetrically, and this element of randomness—a pattern, but a broken one—keeps the design interesting for the viewer. It is also more stimulating to make.

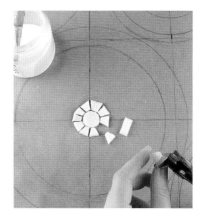

3 **With the tile nippers,** shape a circular tile for the center of your first circle and glue it over one of the intersections. Then cut triangular shapes to surround it. Beginning in the center makes it easier to stick to a quarter tile size throughout the mosaic. If you start on the outside of a circle, you may need to cut fiddly smaller shapes as you approach the center to make the tiles fit, which would look messy.

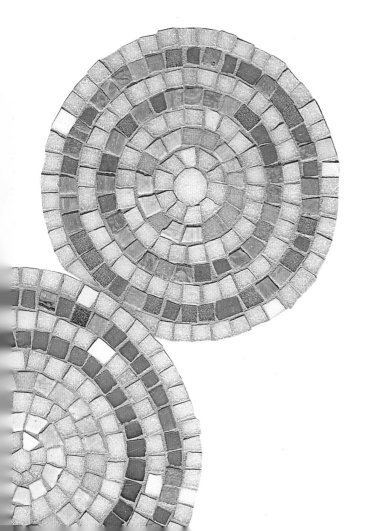

4 **Make creamy colored bands** at the center of each unit of circles (as shown). Occasionally double them up to give variety: a white circle, a cream circle, a white circle and another cream one. Then, work outward from the center, laying alternate bands of color and bands of shades of white. Make each colored ring slightly darker than the one before.

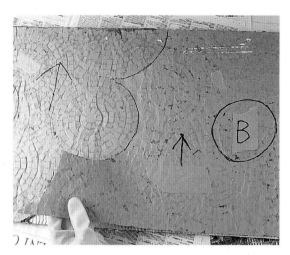

5 **When all the tiles are stuck down,** cut the piece of paper along the outer lines of the circles with the Stanley knife. Then mark A and B and a directional arrow on the back. By dividing and marking the paper after making this design, you can ensure the sections will fit together seamlessly when you fix the mosaic.

6 **Wearing rubber gloves,** pre-grout section A with a gray grout that is light enough not to contrast too much with the white tiles while uniting the tones of the colored bands. Mix the adhesive to a stiffish consistency, then apply it to the area of board that will be covered by section A. Place the mosaic in position. Repeat with the next section. Because of the way the mosaic was divided up, it is easy to see how section B slots into place next to section A. As soon as both the sections are in place, wet the backing paper with a damp sponge and leave for about ten minutes.

7 **Peel off the paper** when it is evenly dark across the entire area. If the paper starts to dry out, sponge again. Once you have peeled away the paper, sponge the mosaic with a damp sponge that has been squeezed as dry as possible to ensure the grout is flat and is not drying in uneven pockets on the surface of the design. When you are sure the surface is clean, leave the mosaic to dry until the adhesive has cured.

8 **Go over the mosaic** with a damp sponge so the dry grout doesn't suck the moisture out of the new batch of grout. Re-grout from the front, filling all the little holes you missed the first time.

9 **Sponge off the grout** and leave the backsplash to dry. Buff up with a dry lint-free cloth.

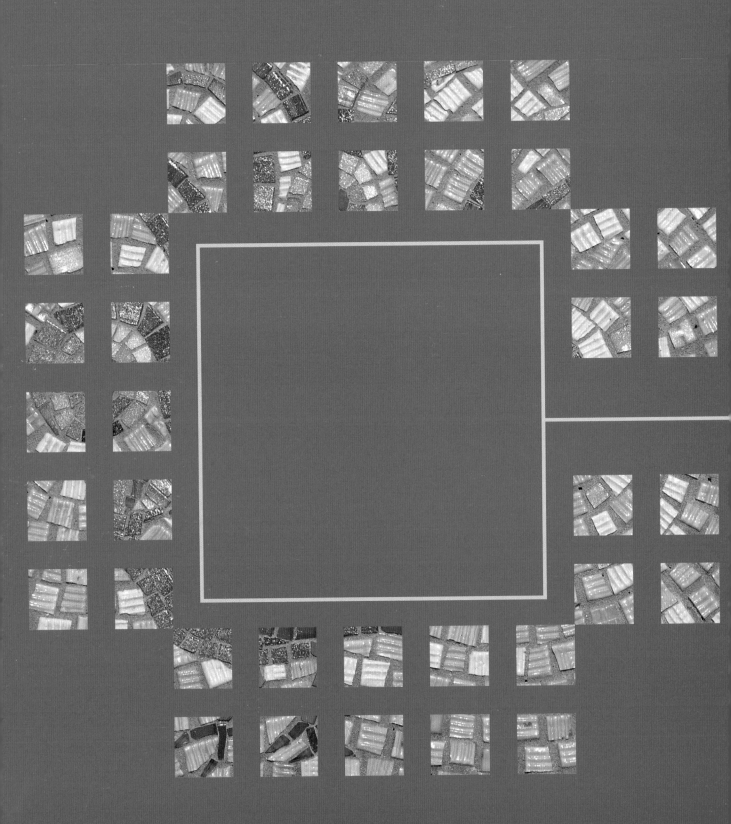

outdoor projects

House Number

This simple project can be adapted for any house number from one to four digits. The black and white design is made more interesting by alternating tiles with an opalescent surface with the plain black and white tiles. When the tiles catch the light, the surface glitters and creates a dazzling pattern. From a distance, however, the numbers read clearly and can be easily identified by mail carriers and visitors.

Because the number panel is designed to be fixed to the outside of a house, it is made using a cement-based adhesive on a weather-resistant board. The simplicity of the design means that it is possible to make it using the Direct Method.

YOU WILL NEED:

- Grid paper
- Pencil
- Templates from pp. 166 to 167
- Tile nippers
- Cement-based adhesive
- Foam-cored tile-backer board, 5 x 10 inches (12.5 x 25.5 cm)
- Plasterer's small tool
- Rubber gloves
- Gray grout
- Sponge
- Lint-free cloth

MATERIALS

- Vitreous glass tiles

outdoor projects

1 **Work out the design** on grid paper. Add a dark border around the whole number and allow about five rows for the width of each number. Some numbers, such as "1," will require less space, and you can fill in the remaining area at the end with a simple pattern.

2 **Cut the glass tiles** in half by placing the nippers at the edge of the tile and squeezing gently. Repeat with each half to make quarters.

3 **Count out the number** of tiles you need both horizontally and vertically. Apply a strip of cement-based adhesive to two adjoining edges of the board and lay alternating plain and opalescent black tiles evenly along each edge. Repeat along the other two edges, setting up the spacing for the rest of the design.

4 **Count out the rows** following your drawing and spread enough adhesive on the board to complete the first number. Lay alternating opalescent and plain white tiles to form the background. Do the same with the opalescent and plain black tiles to form the first number (here, the number "2").

5 **Apply adhesive** to the area where the second number will be. Here, the "3" is in white against a black background. Continue the sequence of plain and opalescent tiles. Repeat for the last numbers (here, the "4" and the "0").

6 **When you have completed** all the numbers, carefully spread some adhesive around the sides of the board to fix the edge tiles firmly in place. This also waterproofs the sides of the board.

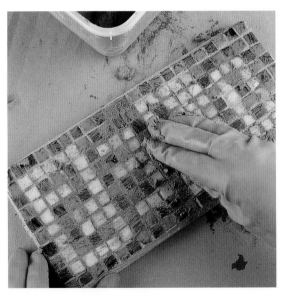

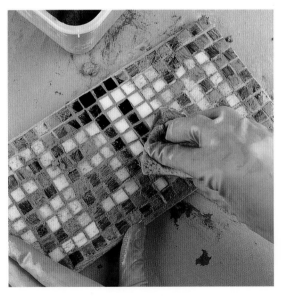

7 **When the adhesive is dry,** grout the piece using gray grout. Do this with your hands protected in rubber gloves. Rub the grout into all the joints, then remove as much excess as you can from the surface.

8 **While the grout is still wet,** wipe it off with a damp sponge, using only the clean face of the sponge so that you do not spread grout back over areas that have already been cleaned. When the mosaic is dry, buff up with a dry lint-free cloth.

These examples show how the designs can be adapted to suit any combination of numbers by using blocks of plain color at the ends to balance the number in the middle. You can also use a smaller board for shorter numbers, but the checkerboard pattern of the different materials adds a decorative touch that would be lost in a smaller piece. A similar but more subtle effect can be achieved by using a combination of shiny glass tiles and ceramic tiles, which have a matte surface.

The opalescent surface of these tiles reflects a dazzling sheen of color when caught by the light. Opalescent tiles are available in shades of blue and green as well as the black and white used in the House Numbers.

Textured Panel

The design for this garden panel is structured around the soft earth tones of marble. The muted quality of this material allows it to be combined with purer colors—in this case, those of Venetian glass smalti—to suggest a color that it doesn't actually possess. This visual trick works so effectively that it looks as if pinks, blue-grays, and yellows have been used. But if an identical set of marble cubes was combined with a contrasting set of brighter smalti colors, the eye would be tricked into seeing an entirely different palette. The panel also contains Mexican vitreous glass, whose semi-transparent, sandy quality echoes a property of some of the more crystalline marble.

There are other design issues besides the color, such as cutting. Most of the circles are cut conventionally, using small squares or rectangular tiles. For the sake of contrast, the large circle on the lower right-hand side is filled with cubes that have more of a curved cut and a more random way of being laid. To give it a visual echo—and to make clear that the contrast of cut was a choice rather than a mistake—the background is also "crazy-laid" (see p. 17).

The finished panel is left ungrouted. This is unusual in a work intended for use outside, but has been made possible by an adhesive that contains a lot of latex, which allows the tiles to move without springing away from the board. Check with your adhesive manufacturer before putting an ungrouted mosaic outside if you live in an extremely cold climate. Frozen water between these open joints could force the tiles off the board. If the mosaic is framed and kept in temperate climates, however, this is unlikely to be a problem.

YOU WILL NEED:

- Exterior-grade board, 40 inches x 2 feet (1 m x 60 cm)
- Pencil
- Pair of compasses
- Long-handled tile nippers
- Plasterer's small tool
- Two-part highly flexible tiling adhesive, for indoor and outdoor use

MATERIALS

- Marble rods; smalti; Mexican vitreous glass

outdoor projects

■ **Draw circles onto the board** using a pencil and a pair of compasses. Cut the marble rods into pieces ½ to ¾ inch (1 to 1.5 cm) long with long-handled tile nippers. (These make cutting marble easier, as the length of the handles gives greater leverage than conventional tile nippers do.) With a small tool, spread adhesive along the outer structural line of the circles. Push the marble tiles into the adhesive, but avoid pushing them down so hard that the adhesive squeezes high up into the joints between tiles. Scrape off excess adhesive around the circles as you work, or it may harden and prevent that row from meeting the next one seamlessly.

2 **Work from the outer edge** to the center of each circle; working outward from the center can lead to the circles looking uneven and squashed. Begin to lay the smalti and marble background. You don't need to lay the background before you finish all the circles, but it will give you a sense of how the completed panel will look. Consider the color relationships as you go. A piece of smalti (such as the pink piece held here) that appears to be a strong color when seen in isolation can vanish into its surroundings when used with marble of a similar tone.

3 **Cut one ring of marble** in an unconventional way (here, the white carrera marble). If you have difficulty working out how to cut the shape you want, sketch the shape on the cube and cut off the pencil line. In order for so-called "crazy laying" to look effective, the tiles should be more or less even in size. Dramatic differences in scale can make the mosaic look out-of-control.

4 **If you need to repair or replace a tile,** dig out the adhesive with a chisel, apply fresh adhesive, and reposition the tile. (Here a gray marble cube is being replaced where an alteration was made.) In the rings inside and outside the one being completed there is a combination of smalti and marble. The blue rings outside the yellow ring combine black and gray marble with denim and gray-green smalti and transparent denim-blue vitreous glass tile. Vitreous glass tiles are thinner than the marble cubes and so need a thicker layer of adhesive behind them.

Right The center of this circle demonstrates how the earthy "red Verona" marble takes on the character of its accompanying colors. The two central pinkish bands seem quite different from the background, but it is only the four pinkish/mauve tiles in the band that suggest the difference.

Right The yellow cubes that stand out clearly when placed next to white marble hardly register as yellow at all when placed next to the pinkish background mix. Color is relative, and earth tones demonstrate this strikingly.

Mediterranean Planter

Terra-cotta pots are made in a range of attractive shapes and sizes, and are a good base for mosaic decoration. They can enliven a patio or balcony, but remember that terra-cotta is not frostproof and may need to be brought inside in very cold conditions. This project uses the most commonly available flowerpot shape and is decorated with glazed ceramic tiles. The tiles are very thick and cannot be cut with great accuracy, so the design has been worked out to use a series of irregular triangular shapes. They have been cut with tile nippers, which give a little more regularity than smashing them with a hammer would, and allows a simple but striking design to emerge from the pattern of laying.

YOU WILL NEED:

- Brown paper
- Pencil
- Scissors
- Terra-cotta pot
- Washable P.V.A. glue diluted 50:50 with water
- Large paintbrush
- Long-handled tile nippers
- Cement-based adhesive
- Plasterer's small tool
- Rubber gloves
- Black grout
- Sponge
- Lint-free cloth

MATERIALS

- Glazed ceramic tiles

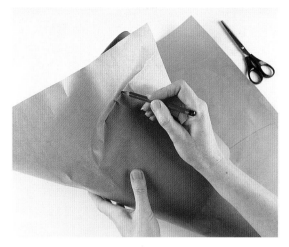

1 **Make a rough paper template** by rolling the pot across a piece of brown paper and marking the line of the top and bottom of the pot with a pencil. Cut a second strip of brown paper the width of the rim.

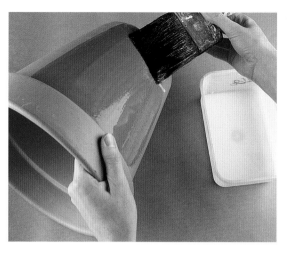

2 **Seal the pot** with the diluted P.V.A. glue. Apply it to the pot with the paintbrush. This will stop the moisture in the adhesive from being sucked out and drying too quickly as you work.

3 **Cut the ceramic tiles** into randomly sized triangles with long-handled tile nippers. The shapes will have ragged edges that will add to the liveliness of the mosaic and do not need to be smoothed off.

4 **Lay out the triangles** on the brown paper so that you know when you have enough to cover the surface of the planter. The rim is also made up of triangles, and these should be laid out too.

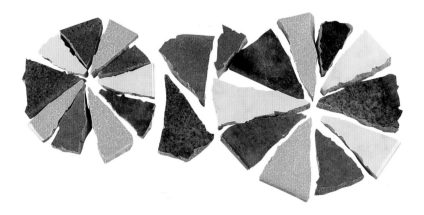

5 **Turn the pot upside down** and apply cement-based adhesive to the terra-cotta surface with the plasterer's small tool. Start by transferring a couple of flowers from the brown paper, then fill in the background between them.

6 **Continue to work** around the pot, turning it as you go. Apply only small areas of adhesive at a time so that it does not skin over before you can use it.

7 **When you have finished** the pot and the rim, leave the adhesive to dry. Wearing rubber gloves, apply the grout by hand. (Because the background is a dark color, black grout is the most appropriate.)

8 **While the grout is still wet,** wipe it off with a damp sponge, using only the clean face of the sponge so that you do not spread grout back over areas that have already been cleaned. When the mosaic is dry, buff it up with a dry lint-free cloth.

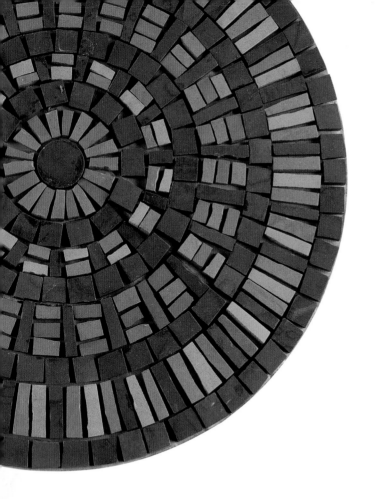

Birdbath

This birdbath introduces a decorative object into a garden setting and provides a useful service to local birds. Any frostproof, shallow dish can be used, but you should position it on top of a post or other support if there are cats in the area. This project uses a simple terra-cotta saucer, sold as the base for a flowerpot. Unglazed ceramic tiles—available in a sympathetic range of earth tones—work well with the color of the clay dish, and the contrasting black tiles create a strong pattern that reads clearly, even when covered by water.

The circular shape of the dish lends itself to a design of concentric rings. The use of a very limited range of rectangular shapes—the tiles get smaller as they near the center—gives the piece an overall sense of cohesion. The color range is restricted to three different browns and the black. The effect created is reminiscent of a woven basket or textile and its simplicity makes it a good project for complete beginners. Covering dishes with mosaic can create difficult and unattractive edges where the mosaic tiles come up to the rim, but you can avoid the problem by leaving the sides plain and undecorated.

YOU WILL NEED:

- Terra-cotta dish
- Tile nippers
- Double-wheeled tile nippers
- Brown paper
- Pencil
- Scissors
- Washable P.V.A. glue diluted 50:50 with water and brush to apply it
- Rubber gloves
- Black grout
- Sponge
- Small notched adhesive spreader
- Cement-based tile adhesive
- Lint-free cloth

MATERIALS

- Unglazed ceramic tiles

outdoor projects

1 **Select your tiles** by placing them on the dish and working out which colors best complement the color of the dish.

2 **Cut the black tiles** into quarters and the other square tiles into rectangles. You may find it easier to cut tiles into very thin rectangles with double-wheeled tile nippers.

3 **Cut a piece of brown paper** and place it inside the dish. With a pencil, trace the inner line of the dish on the paper, then cut out the circle with scissors.

4 **To find the center of the circle,** fold the paper in half and then in half again.

5 **Start sticking the outer black ring** which, like all the black rows, is made up of quartered tiles. With the small brush, apply P.V.A. glue to the section of paper on which you are working.

6 **Lay a row of rectangles,** then another of quartered tiles. Continue to lay concentric rings in this way. Adjust the gaps between the tiles as you complete each ring so that the pattern works out neatly. (Working from the outside in helps keep the rows even.) As you approach the center, lay in the center piece so that you can see what you are working toward. Either use a circular tile or make your own circle by nibbling away the edges of a square tile with tile nippers.

7 **Cut the pieces** for the final, inner row into narrow strips to fit the remaining space.

8 **When the glue is dry,** the piece is ready to fix. Pre-grout the mosaic in black with your hands protected in rubber gloves.

9 **Wipe the mosaic** with a damp sponge, turning the sponge after each sweep. Leave the grout in the joints between the tiles.

10 **Mix the cement-based adhesive** into a thick paste and apply it to the base of the dish with a small notched spreader, making sure that you have a layer of even thickness right up to the edges.

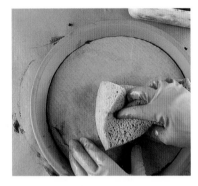

11 **Turn the pre-grouted mosaic** over into the adhesive so that the paper is facing you, then wet the paper with a damp sponge, pressing the mosaic flat as you do so.

12 **Allow the water to penetrate** the paper and dissolve the washable glue (usually about ten minutes), then carefully peel off the paper, pulling it back parallel with the mosaic rather than up and away from it, which would lift the tiles out of their adhesive bed.

13 **When the paper is removed** and before the grout dries, gently sponge the face of the mosaic. This will seem to make the mosaic messier, but it flattens the grout in the joints.

14 **When the adhesive is dry** (or nearly dry) re-grout to fill any tiny gaps and holes, and fill the joint between the edge of the dish and the mosaic.

15 **Clean the mosaic** with a damp sponge, always using a clean face to avoid spreading the grout back over the mosaic. When the grout is nearly dry (after about 20 minutes), wipe the surface with a dry lint-free cloth to remove any surface residue.

Abstract Windowbox

This project solves the problem of creating a mosaic windowbox. Modern rectangular planters designed for windowsills are often made of plastic, which does not provide a stiff enough support for mosaic decoration. Terra-cotta planters are usually shaped in some way or embellished with overhanging rims that are difficult to cover neatly. In this project, however, a wooden box is made to hold an ordinary plastic planter. This means that you can remove the inner box for replanting without moving the heavy mosaic surrounding it. Some windowboxes are visible from one side only, but if you will see both sides of the box (as here), you should decorate both.

The wooden base of the box is drilled to allow for drainage, and the bottom and sides project far enough forward to create a frame for the mosaic, which both protects the edge pieces and prevents awkward corner junctions. Old ceramic tiles with brilliant colored glazes have been used to create the simple abstract design. The tiles are thick so the cutting is quite rough, but the colors are arranged with care and the finished effect is more interesting than a random jumble of broken bits. A project like this is a good way to recycle attractive but damaged tiles, whether salvaged from a fireplace or kitchen or found at a garage sale. The box is finished with a coat of black paint, which connects with the dark grout and contrasts with the vibrant mosaic.

YOU WILL NEED:

- Box made from exterior grade plywood
- Brown paper
- Scissors
- Charcoal stick
- Tile cutter (optional)
- Long-handled tile nippers
- Rubber gloves
- Two-part highly flexible tiling adhesive, for indoor or outdoor use
- Plasterer's small tool
- Black grout
- Stiff brush
- Exterior black paint
- Masking tape
- Paintbrush

MATERIALS
- Glazed ceramic tiles

outdoor projects

1 **Assemble the tiles** and identify the different colors and textures you plan to use. In charcoal, work out your design on a piece of brown paper cut to the size of the face of the windowbox. Charcoal is useful for this stage as changes can be made quickly and easily while you experiment with shapes and composition.

2 **Cut up the glazed tiles.** If your tiles are very thick, you may want to cut them into two or three strips with a score-and-snap tile cutter before cutting them down further with long-handled tile nippers. Long-handled nippers provide extra leverage for cutting hard materials.

3 **Lay out the tiles** on the paper as you cut them so that you can see the design developing and confirm that you won't run out of a crucial color before completing the whole area. If you do run short of a color, adjust the design before it has been stuck down to the box.

4 **Wearing rubber gloves,** mix the exterior adhesive and start to fix the tiles to the box. Apply the adhesive directly to the wood. Some of the tiles are thinner than others, so build these up to create a flat surface by adding extra adhesive to their backs.

5 **When you have finished one side** and the adhesive is dry, turn the box over and work on the other side using the same or a different design. If you choose to decorate one side only, go straight to the next step.

6 **When you have finished fixing all the tiles** and the adhesive is dry, grout the piece with your hands protected in rubber gloves. Strong colors look more dramatic with a dark grout; here a black grout is used.

7 **Because the ceramic tiles are porous,** they absorb the moisture from the grout after it has been worked into the joints. The residue—a dry powder—can simply be brushed away.

8 **When the grout and surrounding wood are dry,** paint the box. Protect the mosaic with masking tape before painting the surrounding edges.

Window Panel

This multicolored glass panel looks very pretty placed in a sunny window. One of the most attractive properties of glass is its translucence. The intensity of color created by light shining through colored glass is far greater than colors created by reflected light from opaque surfaces. You will recognize this effect from stained-glass windows, where the windows glow out of the surrounding darkness. Similar effects can be achieved with mosaic by fixing translucent glass to clear glass panels that can then be placed in front of a window to allow daylight to shine through.

You must select your mosaic materials carefully for this panel: some vitreous glass colors are translucent but others are not. A lot of bright colors, such as orange and red, are disappointingly dull when held up to the light, while others may change color altogether when light shines through them: a dark charcoal gray, for instance, can become a beautiful dark green. The translucence also depends on the chemical composition and firing of the tiles, and this can vary from batch to batch. As a result, tiles that look identical on the surface may look completely different when held up to the light.

This little panel shows how a very simple arrangement—grouping different shades of vitreous glass into blocks of color—can create a lively and interesting effect. Because this piece is grouted with a clear silicone, the joints stand out very brightly against the colored tiles; it is this tracery of pattern overlaying the color blocks that animates the panel. The occasional use of opaque tiles gives extra contrast and drama to the piece.

YOU WILL NEED:

- Scissors
- Brown paper
- Sheet of clear glass 6 x 6 inches (15 x 15 cm)
- Double-wheeled tile nippers
- Washable P.V.A. glue diluted 50:50 with water and brush to apply it
- Clear silicone
- Small notched spreader
- Small sponge

MATERIALS

- Vitreous glass tiles

1 **Cut a piece of brown paper** to the size of the sheet of glass you plan to decorate. Select your tiles by holding them up to the light to see how translucent they look with light shining through them.

2 **Make long, thin shapes** by cutting the tiles into three or even four strips with the double-wheeled tile nippers. This tool allows you to make very straight cuts without shattering the tile.

3 **Stick the tiles**—wrong side facing you—to the square of brown paper, applying P.V.A. glue to the paper, not the tile. The tiles should be stuck firmly to the paper so the silicone you apply in Step 4 is contained in the joints and doesn't spread onto the face of the tiles. If the tiles are insecurely stuck to the paper and the mosaic "crackles" after it has dried, turn it over and paint a coat of glue onto the face of the paper. The glue will penetrate the paper and form a good bond across the face of the tiles.

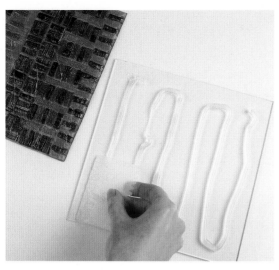

4 **When the glass tiles are stuck** firmly to the paper, apply a thick line of silicone across the back of the tiles, working it into the joints with the small notched spreader. Apply silicone in the same way to the sheet of clear glass, spreading it evenly across the surface to form a layer about $1/16$ inch (2 mm) deep.

5 **Position the silicone-coated glass sheet** on top of the mosaic immediately and press down gently with the heel of your hand. You will be able to see through the glass where there is good contact and where air has been trapped and further pressure is required. Don't worry if there are tiny gaps in the silicone since they won't be visible from the other side. Leave to dry.

6 **When the silicone is completely dry** (after about four hours), soak off the backing paper. Work the water into the paper with the sponge to get through any patches of silicone on the paper. When the water-soluble glue has dissolved, carefully peel off the paper. Wipe off any sticky residue from the front of the mosaic with a clean sponge.

Floral Paving Slab

This little paving slab is designed to be set into a patio or path. It is made of unglazed ceramic tiles, a practical and frostproof material that can be used even in areas of heavy traffic. The design utilizes a subtle range of muted earth colors arranged in a checkerboard of dark and light tones. The colors are not arranged in an absolutely symmetrical way, and it is this slight variation that gives the piece its liveliness. The flowers are stylized versions of common plant forms, adapted to suit shapes that can be cut from ceramic tiles. Some of the petals are cut from whole tiles, while others are cut from quarters and, in the case of the daisy, eighths. Each square is framed with a single row of tiles and the rest of the background filled in following the outline of the design. This gives the piece more interest, because the highly contrasting tile tones mean that the joints will be quite visible. The gray grout breaks up both the pale and dark areas, giving a unity to the finished design.

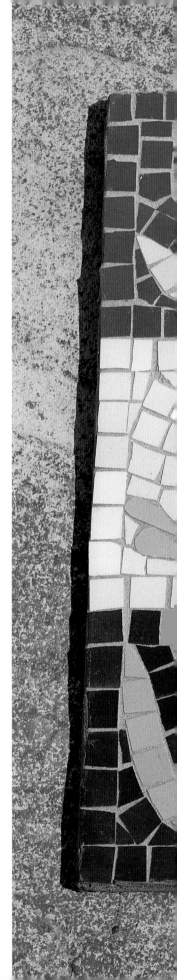

YOU WILL NEED:

- Paper
- Colored pencils
- Template from p. 165 (optional)
- Brown paper
- Charcoal stick
- Tile nippers
- Washable P.V.A. glue diluted 50:50 with water and brush to apply it
- Gray grout
- Rubber gloves
- Sponge
- Frostproof ceramic floor tile
- Small notched spreader
- Lint-free cloth

MATERIALS

- Unglazed ceramic tiles

1 **If you want to make your own design** or amend the project shown, make a color sketch so that you can plan what you are going to do. Arrange single tiles in a checkered pattern to work out a balanced color combination. (A template is provided on p. 165.)

2 **Copy your design onto** the brown paper using charcoal, which is easily corrected. This project is made using the Indirect Method, so remember to reverse the design at this stage.

3 **Lay out the borders** of quarter-cut tiles around the separate squares, applying the P.V.A. glue to the paper, not the tiles. Leave one side open so that you can brush out any debris from cutting.

4 **Choose one square** and lay the flower motif. You may need practice cutting the larger petal shapes. Cut a tile into a rough triangle then nibble it into shape. Remember that only the front face—the side stuck to the paper—needs to have a neat edge.

5 **When you have finished** the flower and leaves, fill in the rest of the background. Try to keep the cutting to a minimum and avoid making very small pieces. It is better to cut a single larger piece than a series of small pieces to fill an awkward space.

6 **When the piece is finished,** leave it to dry.

7 **Pre-grout the mosaic** from the back using your hands protected in rubber gloves.

8 **Wipe the mosaic** with a damp sponge, turning the sponge after each sweep. Leave the grout in the joints between the tiles.

9 **Apply cement-based adhesive** to the ceramic floor tile using the small notched spreader to achieve an even thickness.

10 **Pick up the pre-grouted mosaic** by diagonally opposite corners and lay it face down on the adhesive bed. Press firmly all over to expel pockets of air that can prevent proper bonding.

11 **Wet the back** of the mosaic and leave it for ten minutes so that the glue dissolves.

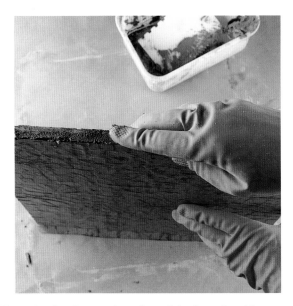

12 **Add adhesive to the edge** of the floor tile with your fingers protected in rubber gloves while you wait. This will strengthen the bond of the border tiles.

13 **When the paper peels easily,** pull it back parallel to the face of the mosaic and press down any tiles that lift during the process. After you have removed the paper, carefully clean off excess grout from the face of the mosaic with a damp sponge.

14 **When the grout and adhesive are dry,** re-grout the mosaic to fill in any small gaps.

15 **Wipe off the grout** with a damp sponge. When the piece is dry, buff it up with a dry lint-free cloth.

The finished tile can be used as a pot stand if you decide not to place it on the patio. Glue a square of felt to the back to protect polished surfaces.

Peacock Slab

This garden slab is made entirely from vitreous glass as an exercise in non-naturalistic and stylized design. It uses the vitreous material unconventionally; the background is laid upside down in order to capitalize on the flickery variations in tone provided by the back of the tile. A dark grout is used to unite the peacock's body and the frame while fracturing the background to energetic effect. The tiles are generally cut to a quarter-tile size, but the jewel-like eyes in the tail have been cut finer.

The peacock eyes are not remotely to scale, and the tail feathers are also not realistic. This interpretation gives the viewer enough clues to read the image, while you—the interpreter—can have fun with the design.

YOU WILL NEED:

- Template from p. 168
- Scissors
- Brown paper
- Tracing paper
- Soft pencil (2B or softer)
- Tile nippers
- Washable P.V.A. glue diluted 50:50 with water and brush to apply it
- Grout
- Grouting squeegee
- Rubber gloves
- Casting frame, inner dimension 1 foot (30 cm) square
- Screwdriver
- Board to turn over mosaic
- Toothbrush
- Sponge

MATERIALS

- Vitreous glass tiles

1 **Enlarge the template** on a photocopier, and use a soft pencil to trace the pattern onto a piece of brown paper cut to the size of the casting frame. Choose colors and cut the tiles with the nippers.

3 **When you have completed the eyes,** work on the purple tail feathers. Make these from quarter-cut tiles angled to fit around a curve.

PROJECT TOP TIPS

Angled cuts are not complicated to make if you follow a few simple instructions. Cut the tile down to approximately the required size. At a smaller size it is much easier to make a precise cut. Cut back from the point, rather than from the widest side to the point. If you have difficulty, reverse the side of the tile nippers you are cutting with. For more information on forming different shapes, see Cutting Tiles p. 14.

2 **Make the eyes** of the peacock's tail. Shade the colors from lighter tones at the top to darker at the bottom. This photo shows the sandy brown ring being made after the blue ring in order to demonstrate the way in which the tiles should be cut. Start with the sandy rings and work inward (with the center of the eye completed last) or you may find that you accidentally produce eyes of varying sizes. Remember to apply the glue to the paper, not the tiles.

4 **Lay the peacock's feet** before filling in the background. Make claws by cutting tiles into quarters, then into narrow points. Lay the background along the broken pencil lines drawn around and across the peacock. If you would like more lines for guidance, draw them in. Place the background tiles the wrong way around—with the smooth side facing you.

When the mosaic is complete, pre-grout it with a grouting squeegee, while wearing rubber gloves. Place it in the casting frame. Fill the frame with sand and cement, following Steps 2 to 4 of Casting on p. 40.

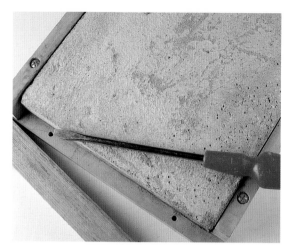

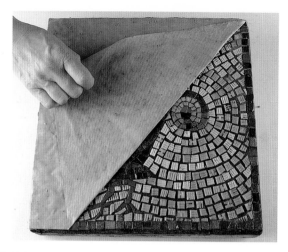

5 **When the slab is ready,** unscrew the sides of the casting frame and remove them. Place a small board on top of the mosaic—now sandwiched between the board and the bottom of the casting frame—and carefully turn it over so the paper face is uppermost. (See also Step 5 of Casting on p. 40.)

6 **Wet the paper** and leave it for about ten minutes so the glue can dissolve. Carefully peel the paper back, starting at one edge and pulling the paper parallel to the mosaic surface, not up and away from the adhesive bed. When all the paper has been removed, wash down the face of the mosaic with a sponge to remove surface grout.

7 **Re-grout the face** of the mosaic. Sponge clean and scrub away any grouty surplus with a toothbrush. Leave for a week in a plastic bag so that the sand and cement has time to set solid before laying the slab outdoors.

Templates

The following templates are designed for the step-by-step projects in this book. The designs that are used with projects made with the Indirect Method are shown in reverse. Full instructions on how to use the templates are given on p. 21.

Bird Mirror Frame, p. 44

Round Mirror Frame, p. 48

Butterfly Tile, p. 54

Dragonfly Panel, p. 62

Pumpkin Table, p. 69

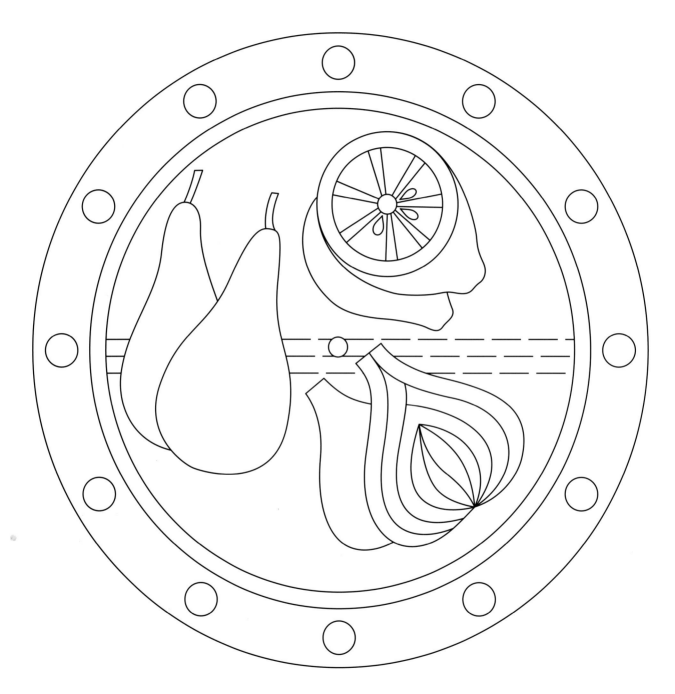

Kitchen Clock, p. 84

Cityscape, p. 95

Patio Table, p. 106

Floral Paving Slab, p. 148

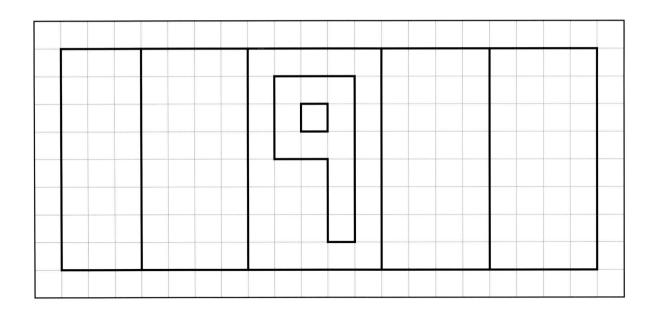

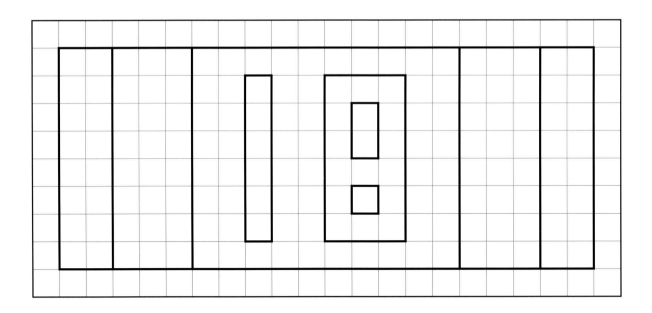

House Numbers, p. 120

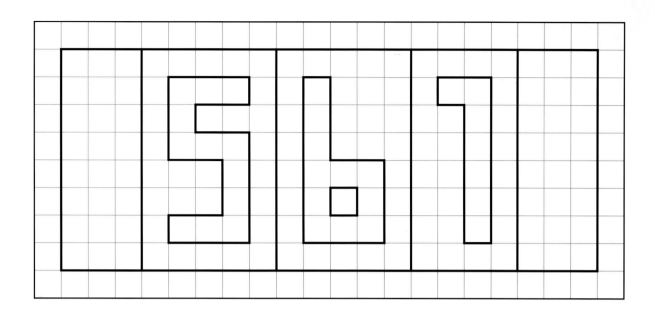

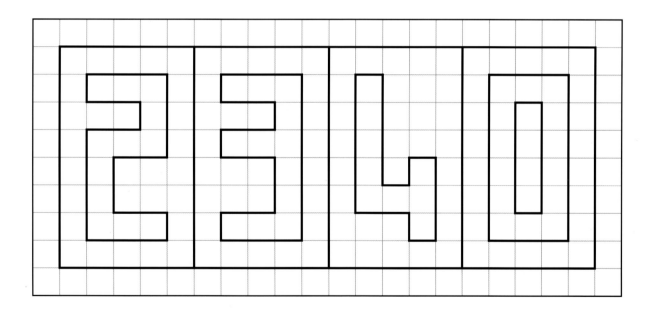

House Numbers, p. 120

Peacock Slab, p. 155

Horse Tile, p. 38

Suppliers

Mosaics can be created from small pieces of almost any material, but tiles of glass, ceramic, and marble are available in packaged form at art supply stores. Be sure to keep the nature of your design and the use of your project in mind when choosing your materials.

Tile Stores

Most tile stores sell fixing materials and tools. Always be sure to check that the adhesive you buy does what you require, for example, since some types are not suitable for outdoor use. Some stores may even be prepared to give you broken ceramic wall tiles that they would normally throw away—don't be afraid to ask for them.

Hardware Stores

These are a good source of fixings, such as screws, pins, and brass wire for hanging your finished pieces.

Mosaic Workshop

Mosaic Workshop, the largest mosaic studio in Britain, was established by the authors in 1987. A second workshop is now open in Los Angeles. Ceramic, glass, tools, mosaic materials, and kits are available by mail order in North America. Courses are held regularly, taught by author Emma Biggs.

The following projects are available as kits from:

Mosaic Workshop
1221 South Burnside Avenue
Los Angeles, CA 90019

Telephone: 917 690 4290
www.mosaicworkshopusa.com
email: sarah@mosaicworkshopusa.com

- Bird Mirror Frame, page 44
- Round Mirror Frame, page 48
- Pumpkin Table, page 69
- Kitchen Clock, page 84 (a version of this using the Direct Method is available)
- Quilt Table, page 100
- Patio Table, page 106
- Floral Panel, page 148 (a version of this is available as a panel for indoors)

In Australia, you can order these projects by contacting: kits@studiomosaico.com.au

In the United States

Delphi
3380 East Jolly Road
Lansing, MI 48910

Toll-free: 800 248-2048
www.delphiglass.com

Michaels
850 North Lake Drive, Suite 500
Coppell, TX 75019

Toll-free: 800 MICHAELS (642-4235)
www.michaels.com

Jerry's Artarama
5325 Departure Drive
Raleigh, NC 27616
Toll-free: 800 UARTIST (827-8478)
Telephone: 919 878-6782 (in NC)
www.jerrysartarama.com

Stained Glass Warehouse, Inc.
2350 Hendersonville Road
Arden, NC 28704

Telephone: 828 684-0211
Info@stainedglasswarehouse.com

In Canada

Craft It Yourself Mosaic Supplies

email:sbenbow@craftityourself.com

Mosaic Beach Studio

1945 Gerrard St.
E. Toronto, M4E 2A9

Telephone: 416-915-1627
Web: http://www.mosaicbeach.com
email: sales@mosaicbeach.com

In Australia

Craftsmart Australia Pty Ltd

4/29 Business Park Drive
Notting Hill Vic 3168

Free call: 1800 100 189

Mosaico Tessera

P.O. Box 1828
Hornsby Westfield NSW 1635

Telephone: 02 9481 0696

www.mosaico.com.au

Studiomosaico

Ground Floor
111 Lennox Street
Newtown NSW 2042

Telephone: 02 9557 9550

www.studiomosaico.com.au

Index

Page numbers in *italics* refer to illustrations and captions. As many mosaic materials and tools (for example, vitreous glass tiles and tile nippers) are used throughout the book, the page references are intended to direct the reader to substantial entries only.

Acknowledgments

We would like to thank Janet Ravenscroft, Shona Wood, Walter Bernadin, Miranda Symington, and all the team at Mosaic Workshop, but most of all we would like to thank Marek Rodgers for his support and patience.